So Super Starry

So Super Starry

Rose Wilkins

MACMILLAN CHILDREN'S BOOKS

First published 2004 by Macmillan Children's Books
a division of Macmillan Publishers Limited
20 New Wharf Road, London N1 9RR
Basingstoke and Oxford
www.panmacmillan.co.uk

Associated companies throughout the world

ISBN 0 330 42086 0

1 3 5 7 9 8 6 4 2

A CIP catalogue record for this book is available from
the British Library.

Typeset by Intype Libra Ltd
Printed and bound in Great Britain by Mackays of Chatham plc, Kent

*For my sister, Lucy – a girl who's
got 'it' if ever I saw one*

I've just finished this book called *Tammy Gets Kissed.* There's a photo of a girl on the cover, all shiny happy lips and shiny happy hair and dimples. Although the photographer has artistically blurred the picture and sort of touched it up with these improbable rainbow highlights, the girl's eyes stare right out at you. They're not shiny and happy. They're cool, hard. They look you right up and down. They're eyes that size you up in a pitying sort of way all the time you're reading about Tammy's crush, Tammy's comeback, Tammy's kiss.

My mother bought me this book. I think it's a hint. It's meant for 'teen girls with a zest for living 'n loving', i.e. moronic thirteen year olds who think maturity is measured by the number of love bites you can collect in a year. My mother would love a daughter like Tammy, who would go all giggly about the 'cute' boys lining up to take her on 'hot' dates, who would raid her make-up bag and run up huge phone bills gossiping with her pals, who would sob on her shoulder when Mr Right went Wrong and then thank Mummy Dearest, gushingly, in her Prom Queen acceptance speech. Maybe she thinks that if I read books like this a transformation will take place: my awkward edges will miraculously blur, I will exude an improbable rainbow glow, I will become shiny and happy. Kissable.

I'd pretend that girls like Tammy don't really exist, only I know that they do. My mother still is one, and when she's on the phone, half the time she's swapping beauty tips and hot-date gossip and acceptance-speech gush with a whole mob of other grown-up Tammies. She's an actress. She's only really known for one thing, that American sitcom about an English aristocrat who's accidentally ended up in LA. *Lady Jane,* it's called. It's been going for years and years now – you know, the one with the snobby English butler and the straight-talking African-American housekeeper and then my mother, who keeps getting US culture all wrong in a cute, ditzy kind of way. It's surprisingly popular, and she does some chat shows and guest appearances and stuff, hamming it up like you wouldn't believe. When you think about it, my mother's whole life has been a performance, a transformation even: Helen Slater moves from Newcastle to London, loses her accent, finds a husband and – ta da! – turns into Helena Clairbrook-Cleeve, My Fair Lady of light entertainment.

It's not that we don't get on, exactly; it's just that we don't *fit.* We don't even look alike: she's small and fair and I'm tall and dark, like my dad. The pygmy blondes at school call me the Obelisk, which is a lame sort of joke about my ridiculous name, Octavia, and my even more ridiculous height (at the age of fifteen I'm a sky-scraping six-foot tall). You see, I'm not sure Shake-speare was right when he said that a rose by any other name would still smell sweet, because I bet my mother couldn't do her Lady Jane thing at the chat shows and charity lunches if she was still plain old Helen Slater from Newcastle. She did her best for me: Octavia is a lovely name – ridiculous, but lovely. Sometimes I would like to cling to my parents' romantic notion of Octavia, the Roman princess, but for most people I'm the Obelisk or even 'Tavia aka Tavy aka Davy aka Dave. I think I marginally prefer 'Dave' to 'Obelisk', though it's a close call. (Look up Obelisk in the dictionary and you'll see what I mean about names marking out your fate. There I am, straight up, straight down, a column or pillar. *Square* and *monolithic*.)

However. Strange as it may seem, in my sort of school I'd be even more of the odd one out if I were called something plain and sensible. Darlinham House is crammed with the children of actors and rock stars and models and the like, all of whom tend to burden their offspring with the kind of names guaranteed to make the vicar stutter over the baptismal font. So in my class the boys are all called things like Zack or Seth or Phoenix, and the girls can be anything from obscure classical heroines to trendy parts of the globe. India and Asia and China. (There's even a Florida in the year below.) It's all an attempt on the part of our parents to mark us out for exotic and fabulous destinies, just like theirs. After all, what Ulysses could ever be happy working at a supermarket checkout till? Could a Tallulah settle for anything less than a lifetime of glamour and excitement?

Darlinham House is a red-brick mansion tucked away in a fashionable square in central London. Since there's no sign on the gate and the whole place is bristling with security guards and surveillance equipment you'd be forgiven for thinking it was a private bank or the head-quarters of a global spy network. The security is offici-ally in case one of my fellow students is kidnapped and held to ransom, either by enterprising gangsters or, more likely, a desperate arts critic, enraged by Mummy and Daddy's crimes against culture and good taste. The real reason for all this muscle is that it makes us feel important. India Withers, for example, is lobbying hard for each of us to be appointed a personal bodyguard to accompany us to class, carry our bags, fetch coffee and, for all I know, file our nails and do our homework for us.

India and Asia are best friends and blonde, blue-eyed Saxons all the way. India, pygmy-blonde-in-chief, reigns supreme among the Darlings, and Asia is her most loyal lieutenant. It was India who thought up both Dave and Obelisk. Today it was the latter – 'Hello, Obelisk, how's the view?' – as I walked into the class-room. My rainbow-radiant, Tammy-girl self flashed back with, 'Not bad, Midget, how's the gutter?', but of course the real me just smiled tightly and went on. India and her posse more or less ignore me usually, and that's the way I want it to stay. But today she didn't leave it at that. Instead, she tilted her head at me in a win-some manner. 'You're coming to my party, aren't you, Davy?'

At Darlinham House, it is social suicide to show sur-prise or shock or even excitement at *anything*. Practically all of us Darlings have at least one C-list celebrity rel-ative and lots are right up there with the A-list. For example, India's father is Rich Withers, ageing rock star

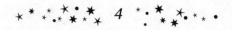

of *Spilt Milk* fame. Zack Fontaine's sister is that super-model-turned-environmental-activist with the long purple hair. Cosmo Jukes's father owns the production company behind all the Vince Valiant films. Calypso Goldsworthy's mother stars in them. And so on. Thus, if Elvis Presley himself rock 'n rolled his way into our dining hall and offered to make each and every one of us a fried peanut-butter sandwich, the most anyone would do would be to shrug in a world-weary kind of way. One or two might risk a raised eyebrow. But that would be it. So when India dropped the bombshell about her party all I did was saunter over to my desk, dump my bag on the floor, sit back and then drawl, 'Sure.'

'Good,' said India brightly. Then, 'It's at Dad's place. I'll send directions.' Slight pause. 'So your father will know where to drop you off.'

I understood this to be an order: India wanted to meet my father.

India is not only one of the richest and most beautiful people in the school (and that's saying a lot), she is also one of the best connected. Her dad has surrounded her with rock royalty from the moment she was old enough to sit on their laps without peeing on them. Her mother, Tigerlily Clements, a supermodel and UN Goodwill Ambassador who jets around the world having her photograph taken with sick babies, has ensured that little Indy has locked insincere smiles with every head of state (and fashion house) worth name-dropping. Rumour has it that India Withers is the only person in the world to have had 'Happy Birthday To You' sung to her by all the Rolling Stones *and* the Pope.

Now, even for an A-list Darling, getting an invitation to India Withers's sixteenth birthday party would be cause for a little discreet celebration. They'd permit themselves the tiniest of smirks, a momentary flutter in the stomach . . . perhaps even a flush of triumph once they were safely out of the public eye. For a D-lister such as myself, it felt like someone had just thrown a bucket of cold water – no, make that vintage champagne – over my head. After four years at this school even I could give an impression of extreme indifference, but all day long I felt dizzy with the fantastic unreality of it all. One part pleasure to two parts panic.

Little girls grow up imagining how Cinderella must have felt when her fairy godmother whooshed down the chimney and – ping! – popped her in a sparkly frock and sent her off to the ball. But in my case it wasn't a fairy godmother but the wicked stepsister who'd just waved the wand. From stay-at-home Cinders to Princess Charming in one fell swoop? Not quite. It was more like being promoted from frog to footman.

I'm not a frog, I know that. I have neatish features and no acne and my legs are quite good, so I accept that there's nothing much *wrong* with me. From my parents I've inherited my mother's pale skin and my father's dark hair and eyes. Plus, of course, his lanky lumbering six-footedness, which would be a lot easier to cope with if I was a) male b) a supermodel c) keen on scaring small children. (Frogs aside, I have a long way to go before I Embrace My Inner Giraffe.) However, having neatish features and no acne is hardly a ticket-to-the-top at Darlinham House, since most of the people here exhibit the very best that genetic inheritance, cosmetic enhancement and designer labels can offer. Even the little twelve and thirteen year olds seem to move around in their own air-brushed bubbles, miraculously resistant to the ravages of puberty or the smudging of lipgloss.

My encounter with the pygmy blondes that morning was the perfect illustration of the differences between an A-list babe and a D-list nobody. I'd left the house in a rush, so although I'd had enough time to dab concealer on a newly emerging spot, the back of my hair was still sticking out in a fuzzy, slept-on sort of way. I was wearing an old pair of cord trousers from PopShop (the Extra Giant range) and a rather pretty pink striped shirt. I looked all right. India, on the other hand, had on a beaded miniskirt in silver satin and an off-the-shoulder chunky black sweater. Her hair was carefully tousled to give that sexy just-out-of-bed look that only comes after hours of primping, and her sooty eyelashes sparkled with a hint of glitter. The effect was glamorous, but with a rock-chick edge. Asia, as usual, was in full-on Party Poppet mode, wearing a cute little shirt dress in powder blue. The slogan stretched across her ample breasts spelled out BONDAGE SLUT in diamanté.

My mother can't understand why I don't devote more time and energy to looking like this. Well, not like a bondage slut, obviously, but like someone glamorous and sexy and interesting. Someone super-starry, I suppose. Perhaps I could, if I started wearing some of the clothes she keeps buying me or took to lugging huge sacks of cosmetics around with me all day like the rest of the girls do. It's not just make-up, either, but all the equipment for lunchtime 'retouching' sessions: skin-reviving spritzers and mineral-enriched facial packs, hair

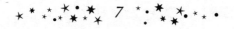

serums, eye drops, nail files, tweezers . . . one girl even keeps a spare set of hair extensions in her locker.

It seems a bit unfair that their male counterparts don't go to nearly so much trouble. Most of the boys here are heavily into the Designer Tramp look: clothes so distressed they're practically screaming, stubble (if you're old enough) and a permanent whiff of cigarette smoke and booze (even if you're not). It's only a matter of time before one of them starts smelling of wee and asking his classmates to spare some change for a cuppa.

I don't want to be a Darling, I don't think I *could* be a Darling. My preference for a quiet, boring, ordinary life is seen as deeply eccentric, unhealthy even. I take pride in the fact that the pygmy blondes and the rest think that I'm a lost cause and I like to think that my refusal to play the game is a secret source of irritation for them. But one of the most surprising – and disturbing – things about India's invitation was how much I was excited by it, even though I knew quite well that if India had suddenly decided to notice me it was only because she wanted something. And I had a pretty strong suspicion of what that something was.

After school I went to Viv's house. Viv is not a Darling. We met in the park when we were both nine and Viv's mother rushed up to mine to ask for an autograph. Ever since her moment of celebrity-spotting by the swings, Mrs Duckworth has continued to see me in a *Lady Jane*-ish glow. She thinks my mother is nearly as classy as forties glamourpuss Vivian Leigh (Viv's namesake) and keeps on asking me when my mother is going to do her first Big Film. She saves me all the scraps of Lady Jane/ Helena Clairbrook-Cleeve trivia from her women's magazines, and tapes my mother's fleeting chat-show or 'guest-artist' appearances. Occasionally, in hushed and furtive tones, she asks me about what 'Mr Cleeve' is doing.

Viv doesn't get embarrassed about this or anything else for that matter. She just thinks it's funny; she thinks my whole life is funny. Funny ha-ha or funny peculiar?, I once asked her. Both, said Viv firmly. Then she said she'd still be my friend if I stopped being funny, but not if I ever stopped being peculiar. She finds Darlinham House the funniest thing of all and loves my stories of 'morning meditation' rather than assembly, sushi instead of chips for lunch, and classes in t'ai chi, media studies and Sanskrit. When she heard about India's party all she said was, 'Whatever you do, don't tell Mum. She still thinks Rich Withers is sex on legs.' Then we laughed quite a lot because R.W. is old and leathery and haggard looking, with the most enormous nose (India takes after the ex-Mrs Withers, alas).

Viv's failure to swoon with awe over my party in-vitation had put things in perspective, if only for a little while. I told Viv about the Tammy book as well. Viv is quite tall, but she's firm and bouncing and *compact*, with the kind of satiny brown hair you can flick around lots; there's quite often a love-struck boy from her compre-hensive loitering in the street when I come to visit her. She's very into post-feminist theory, which, she tells me, is a 'non-prescriptive response to the complexities inherent in the construction of the sexual subject'. Viv has no plans to be a sexual subject just yet, since she reckons that there's no point trying to relate to boys until they're well past adolescence, because they mature so much more slowly than girls. However, she is very kind to her unrequited admirers, and once explained to me that the real obstacle to gender equality isn't men as such but something called socio-cultural conditioning. The Tammy book is a prime example of this, apparently. She says it pretends to be about girl power, but the moral of the story is that you can't be a happy, successful female unless you're cute-as-a-button with a boyfriend to match.

I agreed with her, of course. But I couldn't help thinking how nice it would be to find someone *I* could socio-cultural condition into being the perfect, empowering, sky-scraper-tall boyfriend.

I got home from Viv's just before suppertime, only a few minutes after my mother. She came back from the States a week ago after filming the latest *Lady Jane* series, and now she's doing a detective drama for the BBC (playing yet another aristocrat, this time one of the bitchy, not ditzy, variety). I'd decided I wasn't going to mention the party to her until nearer the date, and then casually drop it into the conversation, almost as if by accident. I wanted to have more time to myself to get used to the idea. Although I'd said yes to India in school, it wasn't too late to find a way of getting out of it . . .

But I had to admit it: I was pleased to be invited, in spite of everything. In spite of the fact that getting weak-kneed about going to an A-list party went against all my principles. In spite of the fact that I would be playing into India's hands just by accepting her invitation. In spite of the fact that I would probably spend the whole night alone, skulking in a corner. And I knew that as soon as I told my mother about the invitation all these doubts would be swept aside in an orgy of congratulation. At long last, Lady Jane's prim, prickly daughter had the chance to air-kiss with the in-crowd – what more could any loving parent wish for?

However, the urge to tell all soon proved irresistible and halfway through helping my mother to put away the shopping I attempted a careless 'oh-by-the-way'-type aside that came out, of course, with about as much subtlety as a trailer for a Vince Valiant film:

> Mother: 'Darling, could you please put the milk in the fridge?'
> Self: 'Milk? Oh, milk! Well, speaking of milk, *spilt* milk, that is, ha ha, I've been invited to this party. India's party, in fact. Er, where do you want the chargrilled artichoke hearts?'

My mother, of course, was in ecstasies. Not for her the minimalist Darling approach; the shrugged shoulder, the raised eyebrow. 'Oh, sweetheart! How super! That's Rich Withers's daughter, isn't it?' Her eyes were bright and her cheeks all flushed. 'Now I'm *sure* Rich and I have met, you know. Didn't he used to live quite near by? Such a remarkably charming man!'

'You probably saw him at parents' evening,' I said coldly. It was embarrassing that the simple fact that I'd been invited to a social gathering filled my mother with such surprise and joy. Or was it just because I was at long last going to rub shoulders with the rich and witless? Or

could my own mother be hankering after India's father, Mr Sex-On-Withered-Legs?

On she went: 'We'll have to get you a new dress, of course. White, did you say the theme was? How clever of India. White's lovely – *everyone* looks good in it. And there'll be all sorts of glamorous people there. Rich always knew so many different people – really fascinating, really *interesting* people – and I'm sure his daughter's the same.'

I shrugged. 'I wouldn't know.' Then, deliberately, 'I'm afraid I can't take any credit for social climbing. I've only been invited because India wants to network with Dad.'

Instantly, my mother's face went tight and lost its flushed, pleased look. 'Really, Octavia! I hardly think that the daughter of Rich Withers is in need of anything that poor Hector could offer.' I shrugged my shoulders again. As I left the kitchen, I caught my own face reflected in the mirror by the door, and there was this horrible little sneer on it.

I know I shouldn't have said that about social climbing and India only wanting to meet Dad. And I shouldn't have flounced out of the kitchen like that, I should have stayed and humoured my mother and talked about dresses and themed parties or whatever. It's just that it sometimes seems as if we're billed as appearing on the same show, we're on the same set, we know our lines and the props are in place – but somehow we're reading from completely different scripts. I don't *want* to become a proper Darling with the shrugs and the smirks and the cool, bored eyes. But I don't want to be a

Tammy, either. I don't want to get giggly and grateful over an invitation that isn't really anything to do with me, but Hector Cleeve, whatever my mother would like to think.

My father is the latest in a long ancestral line of Hector Clairbrook-Cleeves. You can find a portrait of the first one, ennobled in the seventeenth century by Charles II, somewhere in the depths of the National Portrait Gallery. The present Lord Clairbrook-Cleeve lives in dusty splendour in Mayfair, where he spends his time making life unpleasant for the world in general and our family in particular. In spite of, or maybe because of, that aristocratic ancestral line, Dad usually keeps to just 'Cleeve' in his professional life. My mother can't understand this at all and name-drops her illustrious papa-in-law at every opportunity.

Dad's a director. A good director. He mostly does theatre but he's done a couple of films as well – odd, clever, quiet films that win prizes at festivals and starred reviews in newspapers, but which not all that many people go to see. That's how he met my mother, still called Helen Slater at the time, who'd just arrived in London hoping for fame 'n fortune and her name in lights. He was putting together his first film, a short, shot-on-a-shoestring feature about a park attendant or something, and she got a part in it. They were both very young (she was eighteen, he was twenty-three) and they got married, and I came along, and soon after that Helena, as my mother now called herself, landed the lead role in a film called *Lady Jane* – a low-budget but unexpectedly successful romantic comedy about a ditzy young English aristocrat who marries a rascally

American and then gets abandoned in LA. And soon after *that*, my father announced that he was leaving my mother for another man.

It must have been awful. I mean, really awful. I understand that. But my mother admits (to no less an authority than Suzi Sanmartini on *Tell It Like It Is*) that she'd kind of seen it coming. And it's not like Dad found anything wrong with her, as such, or traded her in for a younger or richer or smarter or more beautiful woman. He just couldn't be with *any* woman. She was getting regular work by then, even if the roles weren't particularly exciting – adverts, bit parts in films, bigger parts in TV dramas – and a year or two later the spin-off series from *Lady Jane* got commissioned. Back in England, Dad had made quite a name for himself after a production of *The Tempest* he'd directed in a little regional theatre transferred to the West End and then toured the States. So they were both doing quite well, and they still are, I suppose, in their different ways. But nearly thirteen years after the divorce, Dad's name is still mud as far as my mother's concerned. If she has to mention him at all, it's always 'poor Hector', slid through pinched lips.

Dad's had a few relationships since the divorce, but Michael, his boyfriend now, has been with him for the last six years. He's a lawyer and he's really nice. He's teaching me how to cook and does funny impressions of the actors Dad directs. My mother, however, has never, as far as I'm aware, openly acknowledged his existence and won't even make eye contact with him if she can possibly help it. (I find this odd – I mean, she's always had lots of gay friends and will quite happily spend hours discussing their love lives over coffee. And it isn't as if it was Michael who seduced Dad away from her all those years ago.) She hasn't got a boyfriend, though she does occasionally have 'dates'. In interviews, like with Ms Sanmartini, my mother will say – voice husky with emotion – 'In spite of everything, my daughter's close and loving relationship with Hector is a source of boundless joy to me.'

I usually stay with Dad and Michael while my mother is over in America filming the latest *Lady Jane* series. I don't expect this is a source of 'boundless joy' to her but, to be fair, she'd probably be worried if I suddenly stopped getting on with him. They speak on the phone occasionally, sometimes they meet up to discuss things (i.e. me), but she never asks me what he's doing or lets slip that she knows anything about his current projects or plans or prizes or whatever. So maybe she really doesn't know about his latest film and how he's just signed up Drake Montague as his leading man. I find this hard to believe, though, because even the tabloids have been making a fuss about him now that Drake, Hollywood's latest 'rising star', is making the transition from big action flicks to a small British film to be directed by Hector Cleeve. India certainly knows. India, bless her little gold-plated heart, wants To Act and has doubtless got her beady blue eyes trained on Dreamboat Drake and, as an extra bonus, the artistic chic associated with a low-budget indie film. A film that just happens to be directed by her old school chum Octavia's father.

To understand why India is taking the Drake Montague–Hector Cleeve connection so seriously, you have to realize that India wants to be more than yet another blonde starlet on the Hollywood assembly line. Celebrity is all well and good, but India's after something bigger, better and *much* more exclusive. Credibility. The magic blend of artistry and allure that's not just about drunken parties and a tabloid column or two. It's about statuettes and staying power and people hanging on, breathlessly, to your every word. It's about getting away with whatever you want because everything you touch comes out in a rash of red carpets.

Even I could see that Drake and/or his connections would get India's career off to the perfect start; for one thing, he's young (nineteen) and still relatively new on the scene and so, according to India's calculations, should be well within her reach. However, not only has Drake decided to relaunch himself as a Serious Actor, he's also decided to become one of the mysteriously reclusive ones. You know, the type who won't even turn up to their own premiere because they're in a log cabin writing a novel on the shallowness of celebrity life. And as long as these sensitive souls are careful not to say anything too wacko and continue to make fashionable films and take good care of their cheekbones, with a bit of luck they become even hotter property than in the days when they turned up to the opening of an envelope.

So Drake's major attraction was also the major obstacle to India's plans. If he were just another dumb hunk coming over to dip his toes in Cool Britannia, he'd surely be enjoying cosy family suppers in the Withers's household by now. Instead, he'd holed himself up in an 'undisclosed location', practising yoga, drinking seaweed juice and getting ready to bare his soul in the cause of Art. India's solution to this was blatantly simple: suck up to the Obelisk and her obscure film-making father and exclusive access to Drake and Oscar nominations would surely follow.

My own part in this was less straightforward. I'd finally decided that I did, on balance, want to go to the party, not least because my attendance would make my mother weep with joy. I did not, however, intend to go merrily along with India's plans. As I didn't even know what these plans *were*, exactly, there were lots of vague dreads building up in my mind together with the first ripple of anticipation . . . I wished I could explain all this to my mother in a way that she would understand. But most of all, I wished she hadn't made it so crushingly obvious how much this invitation meant to her.

Except where my father is concerned, my mother is incapable of long-term sulking, partly out of natural good cheer and partly, I suspect, from fear of frown-lines. I try to avoid sulking on principle, because sulking is what Darlings do best, so between the two of us we managed a truce over supper. No further mention was made of new dresses or the Withers's family charm or the sudden popularity of Hector Cleeve. However, the subject was unavoidable once I got to school.

'So, I hear you're going to India's party,' announced Twinkle as we were putting up posters for the Peruvian Pashmina-Weavers' Fund, Year Ten's charitable cause for the autumn term.

'Er, yes,' I said, a bit nervously. Twinkle, I knew, had not received an invitation from India, perhaps because of an unflattering reference to Tigerlily Clements in her mother's recent biography, *The Mystic Roundabout*. (Twinkle's mother was a minor TV presenter until her well-publicized breakdown seven years ago when she went off to grow cannabis in the Hindu Kush. She has since made a triumphant comeback as a 'holistic counsellor and spiritualist to the stars'.)

Twinkle's twenty silver bangles clashed aggressively with each shot of the staple gun. She's got the Boho Chic look down to a fine art; today she was wearing a stripy knitted dress, sequinned headscarf, jewelled flip-flops and a bad-tempered expression. Achingly hip hippies don't seem to be as keen on Peace and Love as the old-fashioned, less-well-groomed variety. 'Well,' she said, with a toss of her henna-tinted curls, 'I hope you don't find it too much of a bore. Once you've been to one of these fancy parties you've been to them all. But then, how would you know? I suppose the novelty of getting invited to *anything* is a big deal for you.'

By the time Twinkle flounced off I was even more determined to prove to the Darlings that I was perfectly capable of surviving a social gathering without wetting my knickers at the wondrousness of it all. And speaking of wondrousness, I couldn't help admiring how India had kept up her air of terminal indifference even where her own party was concerned, yet still managed to get everyone else abandoning the smirks and the shrugs for fairly lively speculation. Whisper, whisper, whisper. Twitter, twitter, twitter.

'They're sending a photographer from the *Prattler*. He's going to do a centre-page spread.'

'India's brother went to school with Prince Richard. Do you think he'll be there?'

'Even the catering is themed. *Everything's* going to be white. I've heard that they're only going to serve vodka and vanilla ice cream.'

'*I* heard that there'll be this big ice sculpture of a polar bear. And a candyfloss bar. And a champagne fountain.'

'Rich Withers wanted to cover the whole street in fake snow and fairy lights but the residents' association complained.'

'I don't know about the fake snow, but they're definitely carpeting the driveway in white roses. Thornless ones. They're going to have to fly them in specially from somewhere in the Middle East.'

'India's outfit's been personally designed for her by Zoë McCarthy as a birthday present. She's a friend of the family, you know.'

And so on.

My main friend at school is a girl called Jess (for Jezabel). Her mother is a pert, perky, ginger-haired woman who stars in a best-selling series of health 'n fitness videos. In Darling terms this is very D-list indeed. We have bonded chiefly because Jess loathes Darlinham House even more than I do, and spends most of her time trying to persuade her mother to send her to a normal school. Perhaps to compensate for her mother's unfailing bounciness, Jess is very quiet, watchful even, as if she's holding something back. She has a smooth, creamy face that takes on a special glazed expression whenever India's around. India's response to this is to tap the side of her head in a significant manner. '*Poor*

Jess. Her mother kept bending and bouncing around all through her pregnancy, you know. Jolting the womb like that – it's just not *healthy*.' Then she will lower her voice and look sorrowful. 'Slows the child down, if you know what I mean.'

I like Jess a lot, but although we spend quite a lot of time together I don't really feel that I know her that well. However, even Jess was interested by my sudden promotion to the Darlinham A-list. 'Rather you than me,' was what she first said, and I knew that with her this was true, not an attempt to seem too-cool-to-care. 'Do you actually *want* to go to this thing?'

'I keep changing my mind,' I admitted. 'But one thing's for sure – my mother will never speak to me again if I turn the invitation down . . . even though I don't really know why I had one in the first place. I mean, I know it's to do with Dad and India wanting to get her talons into Drake Montague. But I don't quite see what I'm supposed to do about it. I can hardly take either Drake or my father along as my guest for the night.'

'What are you going to say to them all? What are you going to *wear*?'

That was a point. I watched Tallulah attempt to light a Bunsen burner while not setting the sleeves of her purple-and-green kimono on fire. Her father is a famous Iraqi-Belgian fashion designer, which might have its drawbacks in the middle of Double Chemistry but is a definite bonus when it comes to strutting one's stuff in high society.

'Your mother could help. With the clothes and things, I mean. She must be used to that sort of stuff. At least everyone knows she's, well, *classy.*' Jess measured out the sulphuric acid with a heavy sigh. Her mother is famous for her peach Lycra ensembles and matching wet-look lipstick. 'I would give,' she said slowly, 'fifty ice-sculpted polar bears and a hundred Zoë McCarthy designer outfits *and* a date with Prince Richard just to leave this school.'

I agreed with her, but though I feel the same way about Darlinham House and its inmates as she does, I don't like admitting that I'm probably still better off here than I would be anywhere else. Maybe Dad could persuade my mother to let me move somewhere different, but a small, cowardly part of me wonders if my mother's got it right. Not about the beauty-parlour/finishing-school aspect of the place ('yes, you too can have the latest in accessory offspring – specially groomed to complement every stage of your celebrity life and career! Rely on us to showcase your gene pool to the best possible advantage!'), but the fact that at Darlinham House my family and its lifestyle is . . . ordinary.

How would a girl rejoicing in the name of Octavia Clairbrook-Cleeve fare in a normal school, a school like Viv's, among people with orderly, normal names and orderly, normal lives? I tried to imagine my parents fitting in with the Jethro Park Comprehensive scene: Lady Jane running a cake-stall at the school fête – actually, she'd probably be asked to *open* the school fête – and holding court among all the Mrs Duckworths of the world . . . Dad and Michael turning up arm-in-arm for parents' evening . . . At least here people would never, ever bother to comment on your mother gushing about

The Joy of A Daughter's Love on some breakfast chat show, because it will be their parents' turn next week. At least here, if you're not in therapy or rehab, one of your parents is, and the fact that your father is cohabiting with another man is no more interesting or awkward than having a mother who is now on her fifth marriage (Cosmo) or a sixty-year-old father with a string of twenty-year-old girlfriends (Calypso). At least here, all of us Darlings are locked up safe in our glasshouses, unable to hurl stones.

The formal invitation arrived on Saturday: a white silk ribbon with just the time of the party and India's date of birth embroidered on it in gold. There was also an RSVP card with directions on the back. India had somehow got hold of my father's address, so the invitation was sent there, and not to my official address at Lady Jane's, which I suspected was a deliberate reminder of where my obligations as a guest lay. I usually spend Saturdays with Dad and Michael, so there it was waiting for me, practically the first thing I saw as I walked in the door.

I told them all about it over lunch – the Prince Richard/*Prattler*/champagne-fountain rumours that is, not the Drake Montague dimension. I wasn't ready for that quite yet. Dad loves hearing about Darlinham House nearly as much as Viv does, and when I related the great fake snow v white roses debate (as argued by Cosmo and Tallulah during Ashtanga yoga on Friday), Michael nearly choked on his soup with laughing. I was laughing as well, but part of me felt a bit lonely. All the Darlinham stuff just isn't *real* for Dad or Michael or Viv, and when I tell the stories and do the impressions and generally take the piss it doesn't seem real to me either. But it *is* real, it's my life, eight hours a day, five days a week, and though I pretend that none of it matters, of course it does. It matters to my mother, but for different reasons, and sometimes I think that's the loneliest thing of all.

After we'd finished speculating about the other white-themed things that might be available at the party (Rice pudding? Sacrificial virgins? Essex-girl stilettos? Cocaine?), I asked Dad about his film. It's an adaptation of some hotshot writer's first novel and centres around a family reunion to which a charismatic young man (Drake) turns up, claiming to be a long-lost relative. Before long, he's manipulating those around him into exposing all sorts of secret tensions and conflicts. So it's a mystery as much as anything – the audience don't know who the young man is, whether his intentions are harmful or good, if he's just a clever con artist, or if his strange powers are supernatural in origin.

They're only a couple of weeks off filming, so all the speaking roles have been cast – bad luck for India – and most of the supporting artists selected, locations secured and a filming schedule drawn up. Dad was still apprehensive about keeping within the very tight budget and about the fact that the actors had only had a week of rehearsals, which is usual for a film but completely different from theatre, of course. Sometimes with filming there is no rehearsal at all. 'Are you sure Drake can handle the part? After those no-brain blockbusters?' asked Michael.

'Oh, Drake's got talent, that's for sure. And brains.

Don't forget, he's been acting since he was thirteen, and it wasn't only syrupy teen shows. He's done some tough, interesting stuff too; that drama about kids in a prison camp, for instance. So we both know he can do a lot better than *Rebel Blade* or *Psychlone* . . . and of course he's eager to get away from the teen-pin-up label.'

Michael looked sceptical. 'What do you think, Octavia? Is Drake up to it?'

'Well, you'll get bums-on-seats even if he isn't. They're even talking about it in school.' Deep breath. 'Which is why India wants me at her party. She wants to be Discovered. Hector Cleeve's new pygmy prodigy. And at the very least she wants the chance to wiggle her hips at Mr Montague.'

There was a pause. 'Have I actually *met* this girl?' asked Dad. 'She sounds terrifying.'

'She is,' I said gloomily. 'Cold steel and candyfloss. She's going to rule the world.'

'Hmmm.' He tilted his chair back and waggled his eyebrows at me. 'When is this party? Saturday week? Well, I must confess I am agog to witness the vodka fountains and rice-pudding polar bears, or whatever it was. I can see I'm going to have to chauffeur you there myself just to get a look-see.'

My mother came to pick me up the next morning. She always insists on collecting me herself, even though I have been perfectly capable of making my own way home for years now. When she arrived we were sitting round the kitchen table in our dressing gowns, having a peaceful late breakfast with croissants, jam and a mountain of Sunday papers, while Michael read aloud a very funny interview with the director of the latest Vince Valiant film. For some reason, my mother always does herself up to the nines when she has to see my father, and this morning she was wearing a very smart cherry-red suit with a little fur-trimmed hat. Glossy lips. Cherry-red nails. She took in our croissant crumbs and dressing gowns and dishevelled just-out-of-bed hair with pursed lips and narrowed eyes.

'Ah, Helena! How well you're looking! Won't you have a cup of tea while Octavia gets her things together?' Dad waved her towards a newspaper-strewn chair and beamed across the croissant dish. My father is unfailingly at ease even when wearing a purple-velvet dressing gown, with his hair in tufts and jam on his fingers. My mother, however, shot a frosty look at Michael hovering with the teapot and a reproachful one at me.

'No thank you, Hector. Hurry up please, Octavia. I have an appointment with my agent this afternoon.' So I dashed around and got dressed and collected my bits and pieces in a general rush to leave the house before my mother was compelled to sit down and share a cup of lapsang with Michael or discuss my forthcoming high-society debut with my father. But as we were going out of the door, Dad came up and took my hand.

'Listen, love, I don't want you worrying about Little Miss Witless or whoever she is. She doesn't need anything from you, and you certainly don't need anything from her. If you are going to go to this party, go for yourself, and then it doesn't matter whether you take it seriously or laugh yourself stupid instead. It's only worth it if you're going to have a good time.'

We drove back in silence, my mother still looking a bit tight about the lips. I thought she must be annoyed that I'd discussed it with Dad at all. But when she pulled up outside our door, instead of getting out of the car she stayed in her seat and fiddled with the trim on her hat. Finally she said, 'Look, Octavia, do you *want* to go to this party?' I felt myself go stiff and scowly. Of course I didn't. Of course I did. How was I supposed to know? My mother closed her eyes and put her hands to her temples. 'Wait. Let me put that another way. Do you *care* about this party?'

There was silence. Finally, 'Yes,' I said. 'Yes, I do.' My mother gave a deep breath, then she opened her eyes and smiled. A reckless, determined smile.

'Right then,' she said. 'Right. We'll show them.'

Show them what? Show who? India? Or Dad?

Normally, I hate shopping with my mother. She likes bright, shiny boutiques with lots of assistants who hover round you like evil air hostesses: all fake good cheer and sneering eyes. She will try to persuade me to get little beaded cardigans and 'cute' little skirts and glittery little handbags that don't hold anything and tight little shoes I can barely walk in. She will waft around looking cool and elegant and English-rosy, while I slouch after her with a scruffy T-shirt and greasy nose and a scowl. But this time it was fun, once we'd got over a momentary unpleasantness when I'd vetoed her plans for a full-length, Grace Kelly-style white evening gown. I sensed that the Withers household would not appreciate that kind of effort, especially as 'dressing up' for anything other than the Oscars is generally considered a bit common in Darlinham House. However, when I mentioned India's alleged outfit my mother perked up no end.

'Zoë McCarthy, hmm?' she mused, a gleam in her eye. 'Then we'll go vintage.' And the next day she took me out of school early and whisked off to this small, dingy shop in the depths of Camden, with fragments of ancient kebabs and the *Daily Sport* littering the pavement outside and fragrant, polished young women browsing the rails within. 'The top stylist at *Stellar!* magazine swears by this place,' hissed my mother in my ear before pulling out a dishevelled white fur wrap from the rack. 'Now, how about this one?' It wasn't like proper clothes shopping, more like going through somebody else's dressing-up box.

On Wednesday we went on a shoe hunt, this time to one of the shiny boutiques, but I was fortified by my success at the top-stylists-swear-by-this shop and even locked insincere smiles with the sales assistant. I absolutely refused to wear heels, so we compromised on a pair of little ivory silk slippers. Although the shoes cost more than the rest of the outfit put together, my fairy godshopper didn't even bat an eyelid. Then on Thursday evening I was marched to Selfridges, where she embarked on long, intense consultations at the make-up counters before finally selecting a pearly nail polish and lipgloss and two different kinds of eyeshadow. I tried to resist the eyeshadow but my will was weakening. We went out to dinner afterwards – Moroccan, our favourite – and got tipsy and giggly. Over dessert we got out all the make-up and admired the little sparkly packets and lovely glossy bottles. Was this the sort of thing India and Asia and the rest did with their mothers? I hadn't realized it could be quite so fun.

Viv came round on Saturday afternoon to try on my new shoes and paint my nails. She warned me that her mother was already looking forward to my career as a fifteen-year-old socialite. 'She says you should write one of those It-girl columns – you know, "my glamorous life with my glamorous friends", and bore people rigid with tales of getting drunk with Prince Richard at parties all the time. Like Tiara Feckless-Simpleton or whatever her name is.'

'My surname may be double-barrelled, but my brain isn't single-celled, thank you very much.'

'Pity. I'm sure Prince Richard is on the prowl for posh girls of little brain – perfect breeding stock.'

'Well, he'll have landed on his feet then. There's plenty of them at Darlinham House.' I sighed in spite of myself. My experience of the opposite sex is pretty much non-existent. Not that I'm hankering after my very own Designer Tramp, but sometimes I feel that it would nice if the Darlinham super-studs took notice of me for something other than walking into a classroom and nearly knocking myself out on the door frame.

'Ah, well. I s'pose it might be hard maintaining that wholesome schoolgirl complexion on an It-girl diet of champagne cocktails and cigarettes . . . Listen, how are you feeling about tonight?' I was surprised to find that I was actually looking forward to it all. 'Good,' said Viv in her decisive way. 'You need to get out more.'

'What do you mean?' I asked, offended.

'You do, you know,' said Viv calmly. 'You need to

meet new people, even if they *are* all luvvies or darlings or It-girls or whatever you call them. I'm always trying to get you to come out with me, to school stuff and things, but you always make excuses. You wouldn't come to the cinema last week or even out for coffee when you heard people from school were going to be there.'

'That's because I wouldn't know anyone but you! I wouldn't fit in, I'd be hanging around you all the time, it'd be like charity, you'd get sick of it.'

'How are you ever going to know anyone but me if you don't ever come out?' Viv's tone softened. 'I wish you would, you know. We'd have fun and they'd all like you. Of course you'd "fit".' She grinned. 'Mind you, if you're about to get swept off your feet by Prince Richard you'll soon forget all about us common folk. It'll be coronets and caviar all the way for you, my girl.'

Viv stayed while I got dolled up. I recently got my hair cut in a sort of gamine crop, only to discover that you can't really pull off the cute elfin look if you're six foot tall with a nickname like 'Dave'. But Viv, wielding the hair wax, artistically tousled it so it looked spiky but soft at the same time. My nails were pearly, my eyelids smoky with stuff from the sparkly bottles. The top I'd bought from the vintage-clothing shop was a silk camisole, ivory, with thin straps and trimmed with antique lace. It felt cool and frail and thin on my bare skin, like the first touch of snow. Very impractical for September, so my mother had insisted on the fur wrap as well, which I wasn't so sure about, but Viv liked. I was wearing the silk shoes with my favourite jeans. They're pretty faded from lots of washing, but they're a good slim fit that make my legs go on for miles, and the toe of the ivory-coloured slippers just peeped out from underneath them.

For perhaps the first time in my life I saw the point of all those 'you are what you wear' lectures from my mother. I had been sure I was going to be twitching with nerves, but the face in the mirror was serenely self-assured. Just for one night I had the chance to be some-one different, live a different sort of life, so when I saw my reflection it was like looking at a highly polished photograph in a magazine or an illustration in a book. I looked . . . good. Not beautiful, not dramatic, not quite like the fairy tales, but *good*. Cool and elegant and self-contained.

I expected my mother to be bubbling over with congratulatory satisfaction, but she was a bit quiet when she came to the door to see me off. Maybe it was because Dad was waiting on the pavement. Then, as I turned to go, she caught my arm, and she had an odd expression on her face – part proud, part rueful, almost shy. 'It can be hard, I know. I do know that. Oh, Octavia—' But she didn't say any more, so I sashayed down the steps to Dad, who opened the car door for me and stood to attention like a proper chauffer, and then we were off, me doing regal waves out of the back window.

Rich Withers's place was in outer West London, the part with sprawling pretend mansions peeping out from behind high walls and the leafy sweep of their pretend carriage drives. Before the big wrought-iron gate opened we had to announce ourselves through an intercom, and I glimpsed a security camera discreetly tucked in the wall. No sign of snow, but there were tiny white fairy lights absolutely everywhere – glimmering within the trees and foliage, sparkling alongside the drive, twinkling all over the facade of the house itself. The house, from what I could see of it in the glittering dark, was a big white affair crowded with towers and turrets. However, I didn't get much of a chance to look, for no sooner had Dad pulled up at the entrance than there was India, who had been standing on the front steps ready to receive her guests, flitting across the gravel towards me.

There was a delighted squeal. 'Davy! Darling!' Kiss, kiss. She stood back, looked me up and down in a split-second sweep of narrowed eyes, and then smiled adorably. You would have thought I was her number-one bestest friend in the whole wide world. It was a truly magnificent performance – I found myself simpering back through a haze of gratitude. She turned to my father, still with that radiant and trusting smile. 'You must be Mr Cleeve.' They shook hands, India bashful but glowing. 'I am *so* thrilled I've finally met you.' She lowered her eyes demurely. 'I . . . well . . . I've been long-ing to meet you ever since Dad took me to your pro-duction of the *Bacchae* in July. We simply couldn't stop talking about it afterwards. Only, of course, I never had the courage to pick poor Octavia's brains!' Sweet, self-deprecating laugh. 'You know, I thought you raised some *fascinating* questions about Euripidean irony and metatheatre. Though I can't help feeling that the cathartic powers of tragedy are diminished once you take the post-modernist line . . .'

She trailed off dreamily, the light of revelation still

shining in her eyes. Dad was mesmerized. So was I, actually. Metatheatre? Post-modernism? I had seriously underestimated the girl. Finally my father recollected himself. 'Well, I'm, um, so glad you liked it. Er, happy birthday! Enjoy yourself, Octavia.' And he was gone.

The two of us stood looking at each other for a moment. It was a mutually appraising sort of look. (Though I was interested to see that the famous Zoë McCarthy creation wasn't all that different from my own effort: a halter-neck top sewn all over with seed pearls, and denim skirt with a swish of white silk in its fishtail train.) Then another car pulled up and India gave another delighted shriek as its white-clad occupants climbed out on to the gravel. But before she swept off to do the air kisses and the squeals she turned and smiled at me again, sleek as cream.

'*Do* go in and join the crowd, won't you, Dave. *All* the gang are here.'

I took a deep breath. Then I squared my shoulders and went up the steps into a large entrance hall in which there was a small fountain playing. It looked like ordinary water to me, splashing away from two springs in a marble basin set in the floor. In between the cascades was a statue of an angel, not a polar bear, carved from ice. She wore a crown and looked a bit like India. The banisters of the stairs that swept up on either side of the fountain were adorned with white roses and more fairy lights; silver netting entwined with white roses and ivy hung from the ceiling in vast drapes. From somewhere above fell a thin, glittering dust of fake snow. Rooms spilling over with people and noise opened out from both sides of the hall so that Handel's

Music for the Royal Fireworks was ineffectively competing with the throb and snarl of what sounded like *Spilt Milk's* Greatest Hits.

It was a new experience to find myself fervently wishing to see a Darling, but when I took the plunge and entered the room to my left, for one horrible, panic-stricken moment I thought, I can't see anyone I know. It was almost with joy that I caught sight of Asia and Tallulah and Seth lounging by one of the windows. They even acted quite pleased to see me, and Tallulah said, 'I like your top,' before making room for me in the window seat. She looked slightly uncomfortable in a Dying Swan concoction made entirely of white feathers (one of her father's creations, no doubt), whereas Asia was squashed into an itsy-bitsy lace cocktail dress. A quick survey of the room revealed a reassuringly random collection of party-wear. Some of the girls were in sharp white trouser suits, one or two in Grecian drapery and a couple in what looked like bridal gowns. There were quite a few boys dressed up in white tie, and one in a toga, though most had opted for a white T-shirt and jeans. I glimpsed one guy, however, who was dressed all in black, and I couldn't make up my mind if this was subversive and daring or merely pretentious.

I knew that out of our own year, only half had received invitations and, apart from some people in the years above, I knew that I was unlikely to recognize most of the guests. I chatted a bit to Tallulah, and then China and Cosmo and Zack and a few others came over; they all looked a bit taken aback when they saw me. Zack smiled and raised his eyebrows and whispered in Cosmo's ear. I knew that I had surprised them with my stylish clothes and my tousled hair and smoky eyes, and it was a good, strong feeling. I'd 'shown them', just as my mother said I would. Somebody came round with drinks, a sweet creamy cocktail called a 'White Russian', which we all drank rather quickly. I had another one and began to relax.

'Look, there's Prince Richard!' said Tallulah breathlessly in my ear. 'Isn't he *fabulous*?' All I could see was a white-clad back and a royal head of blond hair before he moved out of sight again. But Tallulah was staring after him, starry-eyed, and I realized that here was my chance to outclass an expert in the I-can-hardly-be-bothered-to-breathe brand of social intercourse.

'You really think so?' I drawled. 'Of course, I know he's wildly popular, but I've always found him rather weak-chinned. It's the inbreeding, they say.'

'Oh. Yes, maybe you're right,' she said, clearly embarrassed that she'd been caught displaying something other than ironical indifference. She looked at me with new respect and I felt a guilty thrill of satisfaction – I had beaten one of the Darlings at their own game. I had another drink to toast my success and helped myself liberally when a waiter arrived with a tray full of tiny white chocolate mousse cakes. (The waiters were all male with chiselled cheekbones and broad chests, with little silver wings sprouting from the shoulders of their white T-shirts. China was already locked in embrace with one of them under the table.)

Perhaps the music had got louder, but people were now shouting to make themselves heard. Everyone was getting flushed and fuzzy looking. While Tallulah bawled out the story of her crush on her psychoanalyst,

I became aware of a hot, heavy hand on my back. Zack was slumped towards me, grinning in a suggestive but unfocused manner. His usual style is more Pimp Chic than Designer Tramp and even at the age of twelve he had oozed round the school corridors in the kind of sharp, flash tailoring that made him look like a pint-sized drug dealer. Tonight he was resplendent in a billowy ruffled shirt that put me in mind of Captain Hook crossed with Mr Whippy.

'Dave. Davy,' Zack said thickly in my ear. 'Are you enjoying yourshelf?' He was playing with my camisole strap. 'You're veh' diff'ren' tonight.' I felt dazed and curiously detached from things around me. I wondered if this fuzziness meant I was drunk, and though I wasn't at all sure I liked the feeling, it made it easier not to think too hard about anything. Was I enjoying myself? Sure I was. I was fine. Everything was fine. There was a slight throbbing in my head, but more pressing than that was an overwhelming and powerful urge to *eat*. I was suddenly hugely hungry. I reclaimed my camisole strap and got up, somewhat unsteadily.

'I'm sorry. I have to eat, er, go, I mean.' Then I plunged into the crowd.

What I really wanted was chips. I had this vision of a mound of golden chips, glittering with salt, crisp on the outside, hot and fluffy within – the thought of cake or candyfloss or anything else sweet revolted me. Although I didn't really expect to fulfil my chip craving I decided to find the kitchen and get some proper food. Bread, maybe. Surely I would be able to make myself a sandwich? However, finding the kitchen was easier said than done. All the shouting, swaying, laughing people, the cigarette smoke and the pounding music, made me feel dizzy. I began to regret the White Russians. After I'd squeezed and pushed and wriggled my way through another room exactly the same as the one I'd left I came to what looked like an old-fashioned ballroom with mirrors and chandeliers. There were more white roses (surely they couldn't be *real*?) suspended in netting, and intermittent puffs of fake snow so that the people dancing to the band were dusted all over with it, like some kind of heavenly dandruff. It was quite dark, but there must have been an ultraviolet light somewhere because the snow and the roses and the white T-shirts, etc. were all glowing eerily with that intense blue-white colour. I began to feel very strange indeed.

Luckily, the next door I opened took me back to the hall and the India-Angel (now starting to drip, I was pleased to see), and I was able to ask a passing winged-waiter the way to the kitchen. He looked a bit surprised, but he pointed round the corner to a small passage, and once I'd been down that I arrived at the object of my quest.

The kitchen was a large room, all blonde wood and black marble, the kind that is rarely used actually to cook in, and was full of the efficient clatter of the catering team clearing away glasses and reloading trays. They ignored me, so I felt quite able to march over to the towering silver refrigerator and begin my sandwich project. However, before I got there I noticed that someone else had had the same idea: a small man with an untidy shock of greying hair and a glum expression was perched at one of the marble-clad counters, picking at what looked like a lettuce sandwich.

'Hello,' I said. 'Um, do you mind telling me where you got the bread?' He looked up, gestured to a cupboard and sighed.

'But there's nothing to go with it, mind. No butter. No cheese. No meat. Do you know what I'd give me right eye for now, love? A hot bacon sandwich.'

'Me too,' I agreed fervently, carving off a huge hunk of bread and cramming bits of it into my mouth. I didn't think I had ever been so hungry before in my life.

'Ah, but it wouldn't matter to you, love. You're young. Your arteries can stand it. Whereas a nice bit of bacon would be the death of me. I'm under doctor's orders now.' He lit a cigarette with a trembling hand. 'Are you enjoying the party, love?' I nodded, mouth full of Granary Brown. 'That's a good girl.' He looked over to where a waiter was loading another tray of white chocolate mousse and vanilla ice cream and sighed again. 'Y' know, that mousse's gonna be murder to get off me carpets.' It was only then that I realized I was breaking bread with Richly Withered himself.

It was no wonder, I reflected, that the poor guy had a hunted sort of look about him – I'd only had four years in India's company, he'd endured fifteen. I felt much better once I'd eaten the bread and had a couple of glasses of water. R. W. kindly directed me to the nearest bathroom and I was quite tempted to stay in it the rest of the evening – somewhere quiet and private and cool. But out I went, back into the throng, and as I tried to find Tallulah and the others a braying pack of men in white-tie regalia grabbed at me as they danced round the room in a conga. I ducked out of their way, only to stumble into somebody else. 'Hey,' he said and put out his hand. 'Steady.' It was the guest who'd come dressed in black. He took another look at me, smiled, and said exactly what everyone I've ever met always says: 'You're a tall girl.'

'Yeah, well, life's too short,' I said curtly. It was a throwaway remark that didn't really mean anything, but he laughed and looked at me as if I'd said something clever.

'I actually meant it as a compliment.'

'Oh yes? Let me guess: your next remark will be about Amazons.'

He raised an eyebrow. 'So you don't see yourself as a warrior princess, then?'

'Archery's never really been my thing. And the whole point about Amazons is not that they were tall but that they cut off their breasts.' As soon as I said this I realized what a colossal, pointless, excruciatingly ridiculous thing it was to say. Chopped-off breasts? What was *wrong* with me? Not just a giant with a chip on her shoulder but a hair-splitting weirdo too! It's not like I get chatted up on a regular basis (or much of an irregular basis either), and now that I was at close quarters I could see that this one was what Lady J. would call 'dashing', even if the whole black look was, I decided, more pretentious than brave.

He looked a bit older, had dark hair and lazy blue eyes and a lovely curling mouth. And he was *tall*. But now he had this weird expression on his face, so I thought I'd better go and save both of us some embarrassment. I smiled weakly and disappeared back into the crush. However, although the room was less crowded than earlier and I soon found the window seat again, I couldn't see any of the others, so I wandered around trying to blend in by pretending not to be a) bored b) sober c) lost.

'Hello, Dave, you're looking losht.' It was Zack, breathing heavily at my shoulder. 'Let me help find you.' His eyes were glazed and he was swaying slightly; he put out a hand to steady himself on the wall but somehow managed to miss it. 'Whoopsh!'

'I'm OK, thanks. Um, don't you think you should sit down?'

'Only if it's on you.' He pushed his face into mine so I could smell the creamy cocktail on his breath. Zack was very much part of the Darlinham A-list, and I'd understood that he was going out with Asia, but looking at his flushed face with its small, chilly blue eyes and thick pout (which looked a lot better on his super-model sister), I found it hard to see the appeal. Then, before I knew what was happening, he leaned closer and stuffed his tongue in my mouth. It felt like raw sausage. My first kiss.

Not that I had much opportunity to savour the experience. 'Uuuumphgurrgh!' I said, or tried to say, but Zack had me against the wall and was leaning in so heavily it was hard to push him away. Then suddenly, like magic, he was pulled back so abruptly that he tripped over his own feet and crashed to the floor. Standing in his place was the Man In Black.

'Looks like the warrior princess hung up her weapons a little too soon,' he said by way of greeting. Out of the corner of my eye I could see Zack crawling out of the way of several killer heels, one of which had narrowly missed nailing his hand to the floor. So stiletto-tos had their uses after all.

'Yeah. Next time India throws a party I'll bring my javelin.'

'And you wouldn't want to forget your breastplate.' He said it with a straight face, but there was a definite glint in his eye. I took courage from that glint – in fact, it sent flutters up and down my spine. The next moment there was this flash, from someone taking a photograph I suppose, and I was momentarily dazzled. Once the glare cleared from my eyes I saw that he was smiling down at me, a private, conspiratorial smile. It took a moment for the significance of this to sink in – he was smiling *down* at me. Down. At. Me. OK, so it was from the great height of maybe one inch above my hairline, but it was still another 'first' to add to my collection of rite-of-passage moments this evening. 'How about some fresh air?' he asked.

'Sure.' Now the fluttering feeling was brushing all over my skin in little waves of expectation, but I also felt very calm, almost detached, like this was how it was always meant to be.

We threaded our way out to the hall and then on to the front steps where a few other couples were sitting and smoking under the fairy lights. It was a clear night but not particularly warm (I'd left the fur wrap tucked under the window seat), and when he saw I was shivering he put his arms around me and then took my face in his hands and tilted it towards him. Then I felt the heat and softness of his mouth on mine and it was as if Zack had never happened. Suddenly I felt delicate and sheltered and most un-obelisk like. I could almost hear the violins soar and the audience sigh as our raven-haired heroine and her Handsome Stranger melted tenderly into each other's arms . . . a true B-movie moment, with me, Octavia Clairbrook-Cleeve, as the star. And yet there was a part of me that felt quite disconnected from things, almost as if I were a girl in the audience, not the one swooning on screen.

He moved away from me at last and gave me another lazy, conspiratorial smile. It struck me as being rather self-satisfied, but then I was feeling pretty pleased with myself too. 'You know, I don't actually know your name.'

'Octavia.'

'And I'm Alexis. Otherwise known as Alex.'

'Pleased to meet you, Alex.'

'How do you do, Octavia.'

We shook hands formally. Then he took my face in his hands again and tilted it towards the light, as if he was making sure to remember me. I felt shy and wanted to draw back, but in spite of this, or maybe because of it, I lifted my chin and looked boldly back at him. He was sitting in shadow, but his skin was golden-bright in the light from the hall, and his eyes glinted blue under the dark tangle of his hair. My very own Mr Fabulous.

'Do you know that you're covered in snow?' He gently tousled my hair and showed me his hands all a-shimmer with whatever the stuff was. 'You know, I've already seen two people trying to snort it. God, I can see the tabloid headings now – "Prince Richard and Withers Babe in Drug-Blizzard Orgy." '

' "No Use Crying Over Spilt Coke," ' I suggested and he ruffled my hair again.

'Come on, snow or no snow, it's getting cold out here.' So we went back into the hall and sat on the stairs among the flowers and ivy and kissed again and made stupid jokes about fallen angels and melting ice-queens. Down below, things were deteriorating – somebody was ducked in the fountain, then vomited noisily into the roses; the white-tie, conga-dancing brigade were running in and out throwing mousse at each other, and a girl in a sequined catsuit was braying drunkenly into her mobile phone, 'Yah, he's a bastard, sweetie. I told you so. I told you he was a bastard.'

Then my own phone rang. It was the taxi Dad had prebooked for me, come, as promised, to pick me up at half-one. 'Alas for Cinders. You should leave one of your slippers on the steps,' said Alex with another one of those lazy smiles.

'For Prince Richard to find?'

'I was actually thinking of Prince Charming.' He lounged back looking sleek, in no doubt about his claims to the title.

'Well, do introduce me before I go,' I said a little tartly. I got up and dusted myself off to create a diversion. 'Amazonian warrior-princesses never, *ever* forget their shoes.'

He came down and helped me find my wrap ('Did you kill this thing yourself?') and walked me to the taxi, kissed me, but this time on the cheek, and then, just as I'd given up hoping that he would, he asked for my number. I resisted the impulse to leap up and punch the air in Olympic athlete-style triumph. There was a bit of fuss because he didn't have his phone on him so had to borrow a pen from the taxi driver and hurriedly scrawl my number on an old cinema ticket. 'Well, it doesn't really matter,' he said, 'I can always get it off my sister.'

'Your sister?' I asked, surprised.

He raised his brows, then said with the heavy patience one uses when stating the obvious, 'Yeah, my sister. India.'

When I let myself into the dark and silent flat the first thing I did was go and stand in front of the hall mirror. My eyes were a little pink from the smoke and tiredness, but in the dim light they looked huge, black almost, like my hair, and my face was very pale. Tonight I was scrutinizing myself very carefully, trying to see myself as Alex had seen me. How India would. 'Alexis, darling,' I imagined her saying, 'sweet of you to humour poor Dave like that. She must have been *thrilled*. But next time, do try and go for someone more your *style* . . .' I despised myself for letting even the thought of India get to me like this, so I turned away from the mirror, clenching my hands, and instead remembered every second of him kissing me, and how he'd held my face like it was one of those roses . . .

Once again I saw the scene in my mind's eye: the sound of the fountain in the background, the fairy lights, the soaring violins (implausibly emerging from Handel's *Music for the Royal Fireworks*), the exact moment when his hungry lips found mine and bruised them with the soft impatience of his kisses . . . Hang on. That wasn't me and Alex – that was Tammy and what's-his-face. T. J. How had they got into my romance? And how could kisses be soft *and* bruising? I tried to get back to my soft-focus, technicolour vision of Alex among the roses, but it bothered me that I couldn't remember whether T. J. was Tammy's One True Love or Wicked Seducer. And what's so wrong with giving way to a bit of seducing? I asked myself defiantly. It's a lot more fun than being a drippy ice-angel all your life.

I don't even remember getting into bed, but when I woke up all thoughts of Tammy, T. J. and India had gone and I couldn't stop smirking. I turned on my mobile 'just in case' and found that I was humming along in the shower to *Music for the Royal Fireworks*. Then I bounced into the kitchen and, without waiting to be asked, gave my mother a blow-by-blow account of the guests, the clothes, the food, the music and the decor at the party (everything except Alex, in fact). She gave me a sidelong glance or two but she held her peace. I telephoned Dad and Michael and described the whole affair all over again. Finally I went round to Viv's, where the real assessment began. She revelled in it all, especially the bit when Zack was flung to one side and the Man in Black stood there in all his broodingly handsome splendour. However, she could hardly believe I hadn't realized who Alex was.

'But Alex isn't *anything* like his sister,' I protested. 'No, really. He's tall, for one thing and, um—'

'I see: Alex is the Ying to India's Yang. He's tall, she's short; he's dark, she's blonde . . . so she's a cow and he's compassionate?'

'Something like that,' I said, giggling in spite of myself.

Viv was also full of questions – How old was he? Was it true that he was best friends with Prince Richard?

Did he want to be a rock star, like his dad? I realized that I didn't have many answers, though I remembered that Alex had mentioned doing some kind of work placement in the 'industry' (presumably the music, not the manufacturing one). I explained that he was taking a year off between finishing school and starting university.

'He went to *finishing school*?' She could hardly speak for laughing. 'Where they teach flower arranging and how to get out of a Porsche without showing your knickers? Is Alex out to catch himself a posh husband, then?'

'Not Finishing School – *leaving* school, I mean,' I said impatiently. 'Alex used to be at boarding school.'

'Boarding schools are nearly as weird as finishing schools. He must be a real tearaway if his sex-and-drug-fiend dad couldn't cope with him at home,' she observed, only half joking. 'Maybe Alex drove his father to lettuce sandwiches.'

Telling Viv the story of how Alex rescued me from Zack was a reminder of the possible complications of what she insisted on calling my Night of Passion; I hoped, uncomfortably, that Zack was too drunk to remember our encounter and that Asia didn't get wind of it. Viv dismissed this and the India-Alex issue with an airy wave of her hand. 'They'll all just have to get used to the new, irresistible you. Femme fatale Amazonian princesses don't let pygmy blondes and their chauvinist pig side-kicks get in their way.' I wanted to agree with her, but I knew that whether Alex called or not, the next week was not going to be an easy one.

*

Another of the unwritten Darlinham rules is that no one ever publicly discusses a social event after it happens, so on Monday morning it was almost as if the last few weeks of speculation and anticipation had never been. India kept to her scarily exquisite self and paid me no more attention than usual, even though I was half expecting some hint as to the next stage of her Drake Montague campaign. But the one time I made accidental eye contact with Asia put paid to any hopes that my run-in with Zack had passed unnoticed. At any rate, during break time and lunch she and Zack were seated as far apart as they possibly could be without passing out of India's magic circle altogether.

There was another consequence of my Saturday-night exploits I hadn't quite bargained on: sharing saliva with someone in the A-list had apparently moved me up a notch or two in the sex-appeal scale. I knew something was up when Phoenix, who hadn't even been at the party, lowered his turquoise-tinted wrap-around shades to look me over and then drawled, 'Hi, doll,' as he swung past me in the corridor. (I'm not sure I like 'doll' any better than 'Dave', but since Phoenix probably doesn't even know my real name, I guess this could be classed as a step forward.) Cosmo held the door open for me at the end of Sanskrit and Seth actually *winked* at me as he followed Asia into lunch.

Part of me deeply resented this – what, so now India's brother had noticed me it was OK for the rest of the Alpha males to maybe, just *maybe*, reassess my pulling potential? And yet part of me felt a sneaking satisfaction, in spite of myself. I also wondered how things would be if the impossible happened and I became Alexis Withers's Official Girlfriend and – even less likely – India gave her blessing to the union. I tried to imagine having a girlie heart-to-heart with Calypso during a French manicure or swapping amusing boyfriend-centric anecdotes with Tallulah over a Bellini or three. I would be friendly, but a little distant with them, I decided – after all, Alex and I were independent spirits and held ourselves apart from the rest of the herd. Meanwhile, the Darlinham males would start to wonder what they ever saw in the pygmy blondes . . . I had to admit it was a seductive fantasy.

After lunch was one of my least favourite classes in Darlinham House: Personal Development. Viv says they have this at her school too, when they watch drama-documentaries to warn you off illegal/undesirable activities and then have issue-led group discussions. Since sex, drugs and rock 'n roll have advanced many of our parents' careers (and thus funded our school fees), Darlinham House tactfully confines Personal Develop-ment to 'Finding the inner you, yeah?'. Last term we tried primal screaming and feng shui'd the common room in our quest for spiritual enlightenment. Today we were going to take it in turns to interpret each other's dreams with the help of a little watered-down Freudian psychoanalysis.

Dr Tristram ('call me Trist') Bennet, our resident Individual Empowerment Consultant, flashed his tooth-paste-ad smile, ran his hands through his romantically dishevelled locks and said he hoped we'd 'had a ball' researching Freud's theory of the unconscious over the past week. He organized us into pairs and distributed 'Trist's Tips for Dream Decoding' with a cheery wink.

'Now keep it clean, guys. Save the dark stuff for your therapists, yeah?' Then he stretched out on the purple couch he always has brought in for our classes. His occupation of the couch is a 'Kinda ironic, yeah?' statement about the power play between patient and analyst, apparently. The couch also happens to be a much more comfortable place for a mid-afternoon snooze than an upright desk chair.

I was paired with Zack. Wonderful. Much to my annoyance, I found myself blushing when he sauntered over wearing his usual expression of chilly indifference – surely *he* should be the one acting embarrassed, not me? There was a moment or two of excruciating silence while I stared down at Trist's Tips and Zack examined his nails.

'You start,' he finally said.

'No, you.'

'Ladies first.'

'Very gallant of you, but we're not queuing for a lifeboat.'

'What's the matter, Dave? 'Fraid your dreams are too hot to handle?' He leaned forward and smirked suggestively. 'C'mon, you can tell me. Does Alex make a guest appearance?'

'*Fine*,' I snapped. 'I'll go first. Anything's better than the sewer that must be your subconscious.' I took a deep breath, searching frantically for something so bland and boring it defied interpretation.

'OK, so last night I dreamed . . . uh . . . I went for a walk. On a hill. Then I, er, sang a song. It was a sunny day. I brushed my hair . . . um . . .' Thoughts of Freud had broken my nerve. Suddenly everything I thought of was a symbol for some weird sexual obsession or creepy complex. Zack was grinning.

'So you *mounted* a hill, did you?'

It was at this point I realized that if I had to sit and listen to Zack for one moment longer my fists would itch to smash into those thick lips of his. I compromised by walking away in a dignified manner – luckily for my getaway, Twinkle was taking up all Trist's attention with an incredibly long and incredibly confusing account of some incredibly boring dream she'd once had. Most people had taken advantage of this distraction to continue whatever they were doing or discussing over lunch, so I was able to slump down next to Jess with a sigh of relief. She gave me a curious look but didn't ask any questions. Then India's voice could be heard rising above the general hum:

'Of course, Lex is a *terrible* influence on me. That bad boy's always trying to make his baby sister do *such* naughty things! He says it's his duty to educate me, but I think we all know what sort of education *he's* got in mind . . .'

Asia chimed in. 'I bet Lex must attract all sorts of *desperate* girls.' She shot a malevolent glance in my direction.

'Oh, I know,' said India. 'They're always swarming around the poor boy like *flies!*' Cue gales of laughter on all sides.

'Lex?' whispered Jess. 'As in Lex Luthor? Trust India's brother to be named after an evil criminal mastermind. Did you meet him at the party? What's he like?'

I shrugged. I wasn't feeling up to explaining the

whole business, at least not while the pygmy blondes were in earshot. There were some other aspects of my performance on Saturday that I didn't want to go into either – like all those White Russians and my little tête-à-tête with Tallulah, for example. I didn't want Jess to think I was a wannabe Darling after all. 'He was quite hard to miss. He came dressed all in black,' I muttered.

'You see!' said Jess, pleased. 'He *is* an evil criminal mastermind then!'

Criminal mastermind or not, Alex didn't call on Monday. Or Tuesday. Or Wednesday. Or Thursday. I tried to block out romantic memories of snow and roses and tell myself that this was a good thing – that seeing him again would just cause angst and embarrassment. OK, so he was glamorous, handsome, popular and rich . . . and therefore, I told myself sternly, the pygmy blondes were probably right and he had all the signs of being Prince Just A Bit Too Charming. Lex Luthor. The Man In Black. Then I started to obsess about why he hadn't called – had he just thought better of it, lost interest, been distracted by something/someone else? *Could* someone like him ever be seriously interested in someone like me? Had he discussed it at all with India? Had they laughed over me, *pitied* me, together? I tried to console myself with the hope that India was sufficiently displeased by my exploits at her party to abandon her pursuit of the Hector Cleeve/Drake Montague connection. Then, late on Friday evening, Alex called.

'Hi, Octavia?' It was a fuzzy connection, with lots of background noise – sounded like a party. 'It's Alex.'

'Oh, hi!' I strove to sound unfussed and breezy.

'Look, a crowd of us are in the Rah Bar –' lots of background shouts and laughter '– are you going out tonight?'

'Er . . .' I wasn't about to explain that I was currently slumped in front of the television in my Winnie-the-Pooh pyjamas. 'No firm plans.'

'OK. Why don't you come and join us?' There was a pause while he said something to somebody on the other end. Scraping chairs and more laughter. 'You know where we are, right?' I did, thank God, since the bar in question happened to be right by the boutique where I'd found my shoes.

'Sure. It's not far – I'll be there in twenty minutes.'

'What?' The fuzzy line was getting worse.

'TWENTY MINUTES.'

'Fine. I'll—' and the line went dead.

I had a moment of pure panic. This was not what I wanted at all: a party of Alex's friends, all likely to be frighteningly old, cool and beautiful, probably with India in tow, and me with less than twenty minutes to transform myself from pyjama-clad super-slob to sophisticated girl-about-town. I ran to my room and started flinging clothes about the place with the desperation of defeat. There's nothing wrong with my clothes, exactly, they're nice and they're comfortable . . . but nice and comfortable won't Take You Places, as Lady Jane keeps telling me. At this thought, inspiration struck – my mother was out for the evening. Wasn't she always trying to get me to 'have a rummage' through her wardrobe? No chance of fitting into skirts or trousers but my jeans would be OK and surely I could fit into one of her tops . . . I wasted precious minutes stuffing myself into a sparkly red number too large in the chest and too short in the arm. Finally I found a clingy black cashmere sweater and a black lace vest-top that looked all right. I managed to scrawl a note to my mother to let her know that I was 'out with school friends – back late – taking mob', in between disentangling my bra strap. Then I rushed to the bathroom, had a ten-second wash, brushed my teeth, tousled my hair up again with the wax, and smeared some of the smoky eye-shadow on my lids. With my black top, ruffled hair and pale face I looked like a Goth. So I rubbed most of it off again and clawed through my drawers looking for a belt my mother had given me last Christmas – a Barbie doll's delight; thin, with pink sequins. I made it out of the flat just after nine-fifteen, and was at the bar only half an hour after Alex telephoned.

It was easy to find his 'crowd', since they were the largest and noisiest party in the room and had clearly been drinking for some time. But it took me a few moments to catch Alex's attention and I hovered (or rather towered) at the edge of the group, feeling stiff and exposed. I was suddenly terrified that he'd have second thoughts about inviting me once he saw what I looked like without a flattering backdrop of fountains and fairy lights. It didn't help that he was in animated conversation with a pretty, pouty sort of girl in an extremely short suede skirt, but when he did see me he caught at my hand to pull me over and kiss me on the cheek, only we blundered, so it landed more on my jaw. 'Well done,' he said. 'Meet the others.' I forgot their names as soon as he said them, though I did take in the news that India would be along later. I tried to look suitably thrilled. 'You,' he said, eyeing me in speculative sort of way, 'need to catch us up. I'll get some drinks.'

He went off to the bar, and I was left with the girl in the suede skirt, who I think called herself LeeLee (though it was hard to tell since she spoke with the poshest accent I've ever heard – like the death-bray of a strangled pony). We exchanged smiles without much enthusiasm. The other four in the group were all male, and I thought I recognized one or two from the conga-dancing and mousse-throwing brigade at the party. I guessed they must be school friends of Alex's who were also taking a year off before university. They all had sleepy eyes and bored smiles and were discussing how to bring backpacking up to date through a fug of cigarette smoke.

'You can't do the Far East any more. Too banal.'

'Cambodia's still quite chic.'

'What about 'Nam?'

'Only if you can put up with ageing hippies every-where.'

Alex returned with the drinks, which were rather nasty purple-coloured cocktails. I uneasily remembered the White Russians, but had a strong feeling that all this was going to be much easier if I had something to drink. I soon found myself chucking ice cubes around with the rest of them and laughing quite a lot, encouraged by the fact that Ms Micro-Skirt had gone to sit on someone's lap and Alex had flung a lordly arm round the back of my chair. He looked every bit as delectable as I'd remem-bered and was wearing a pale-blue shirt, immaculately laundered but slightly frayed along the collar and cuffs. I thought, contemptuously, of the flashy suits or designer-label grunge paraded by Zack and Cosmo and the rest of them. Viv and her post-feminist theories were *so* right – if you wanted a relationship with style and maturity you obviously had to go for the Older Man.

After my third drink I grew flushed and hot and took off the cashmere sweater; the neckline of the lace top was cut lower than I'd first realized but by now I didn't care. When I went off, a little unsteadily, to find the ladies', I could sense the nudges and winks going on behind me between Alex and his friends; there was laughter, too, but I didn't care about this either because I knew what this kind of laughter meant. It was congratulatory.

There'd been a moment or two when I'd felt bewilderingly out of my depth – who on earth *were* all these people and what was I doing with them? – but now I felt in control again. Alex had called me, just like he said he would, and here I was being shown off to his friends while he bought me drinks and put his arm around my chair and gave me secret smiling looks, as if he and I shared something private. It didn't matter any more about the sourness of the cocktails or the cigarette smoke stinging my eyes or these strangers with their cool, superior smiles . . . sometime soon, maybe, it would just be Alex and me talking in a corner, not in a late-night bar, but in a quiet coffee shop somewhere. Perhaps we'd be strolling in a park. 'Octavia,' he'd say, looking deeply into my eyes, 'the moment I saw you I knew that you were someone different, someone *special*. My wicked sister has done her best to lead me astray, but here is my chance to break free and prove myself to be truly worthy of you, my raven-haired Amazonian princess.' Or words to that effect.

But when I got back from the toilets India was there, kissing everybody to a chorus of delight on all sides. I'm not sure if she was expecting me; at any rate, she shot me a slightly startled, indignant sort of glance. She and LeeLee greeted each other like long-lost sisters, though I eventually got a kiss too. 'Oh *hello*, Dave. I hardly recognize you these days! Are you doing something new with your face or something?'

'Dave?' asked LeeLee, amused. India raised her voice to carry through the din.

'*Everyone* always calls her Dave, you know.'

'Rally?' asked LeeLee. 'I do find nicknames *such* fun!' She turned to look me over again. 'You know, you're orfly lucky to be so tall. A friend of mine who's nearly as huge as you ectually hess to shop for men's trousers because the gals' styles aren't long enough . . . Do you heff to shop for men's trousers, Dave?' she enquired sweetly.

'No. And Octavia's fine,' I muttered, slouching back into my chair.

'*Very* fine. A very fine girl indeed.' Alex's voice was only slightly slurred. He had had his back to us and was talking to someone else, but now he turned towards me again and ran his finger up and down my arm, giving me a soft, secret look from under his lashes. LeeLee pouted sulkily. 'Now that Indy's here, shall we go on somewhere? Maybe a club?' I finished the last of my drink – now that Indy was here the only place I wanted to go was wherever she was not. However, I was damned if she and WeeWee (as I preferred to think of her) were going to scare me off. I'd shown them once and I'd show them again. I stood up – I had to steady myself on the back of the chair – and smiled at India, my most dazzling and determined smile.

'Oh yes, let's. We didn't really get a chance to dance at the party, did we, Alex?'

Alex winked broadly at his friends. 'Right you are. Let's go then.'

I was in for it now. My mother's face swam before me, her blue eyes pooling with tears, bottom lip trembling with emotion. 'My sweet innocent baby! Drunken! Degenerate! Ruined forever! Life will never be the same!' Or, more likely, those blue eyes were already blazing with rage – perhaps even now she was fitting a lock on my door and booking me into a Teenage Tearaway Rehabilitation Programme . . . Never mind, I told myself firmly, I'd come this far and I was doing fine. Everything was under control.

Before we went we all had to down another round of drinks (which Alex paid for again with a flourish of his gold credit card). I found it extraordinarily difficult to walk the length of the bar and out on to the street without crashing into something I shouldn't, but I gritted my teeth and desperately concentrated on putting one foot in front of the other in a ladylike manner. My feet seemed very far away and hardly connected to me at all – like they belonged to a puppet I was trying to control with rather tangled strings. Not that Alex and Co. were doing any better, but I wasn't about to give India any ammunition for Monday-morning anecdotes.

As we turned a corner, away from the main street,

my new-found recklessness momentarily deserted me and I clutched at Alex – 'Will they let me in? To the club, I mean? They're bound to see I'm underage.'

'No worries,' he said, smiling down on me, 'the manager's a mate of mine. I'll take care of you.' He touched my cheek gently. 'I promise.'

From then on things are vague: I dimly remember everybody cheering as one of our party vomited noisily in the gutter, and a brief twinge of apprehension as I tottered past the bouncers into a dark, crowded club, which could have been any club, anywhere. Alex had some more drinks, and though there was hardly room to dance he pressed me to himself and we rocked back and forth in the heat and smoke and flashing, flying fragments of light that bounced across the walls and faces and still sparkled and swam in my head after I closed my eyes. It felt wonderful to be held by him in the midst of that anonymous crush, to just stand there swaying, not thinking, not trying, not doing, just being held.

I was very tired; too tired even to feel properly drunk. After a while I became aware that Alex was trying to say something to me but his voice seemed to come from a very long way off. I finally understood that he wanted to leave, so we squeezed out (managing to avoid a formal farewell to India, WeeWee and Co., all still braying by the bar) and somehow found a free taxi. I had to help Alex into the cab as he was stumbling all over the place, but once we were both inside he kissed me – clumsily but with increasing enthusiasm. Once the taxi pulled up outside my flat he got out too and let it drive off, somewhat to my dismay.

'Thanks for tonight, I had a good time.' My voice sounded girlish and insincere. 'Um. I'd better go now.'

'You're sweet,' he said, smiling down at me. Sweet? Amazonian princesses aren't sweet. Puppies are sweet, and teddy bears, and well-behaved children . . . It was a knowing, indulgent sort of smile, and I felt clumsy and childish as I tried to disengage from his arms.

'My mother's in tonight. I'll have to sneak in so's not to disturb her. I have to go.'

'I'll miss you.' His hand slid up under my top and rested just above my waist. It was cool on my flesh and his mouth was hot on my ear, and there was a warm, melting feeling in my midriff as he kissed me again.

'Wait. Alex. We're in the middle of the street . . . someone might—'

'Shush, shush. Davy – Octavia, I mean. Sweet Octavia . . . Come here. You're not going to be all prim and proper, are you?'

'It's not that I . . . it's only because—' The warm feeling hadn't lasted. I was tired and dizzy and cold. Alex didn't seem to be feeling the early-morning chill – in fact, it seemed to have sobered him up. He looked alert and assured again. His eyes were shining in the cold half-light and he had a kind of frosty sparkle about him.

'I just want to say a proper goodbye, that's all.' He was half teasing, half serious as he reached to stroke back my hair. 'You're lovely in the moonlight. All glimmering.'

I had to laugh at this. 'Moonlight? In central London?'

'OK, streetlamp-light then. You look lovely in orange.'

After that it was easy to say a cheerful goodbye. Alex said he wanted to walk for a bit and 'get some night breezes' into his lungs before calling another taxi and I watched him go down to the end of the street. I was propped inside the door, swaying slightly, but he walked along briskly, very upright, very sure, his face glowing and his breath turning silvery in the air.

The next morning I woke up early after only a few hours of muddled, rather sinister dreams. I had a sour taste in my mouth and my face in the mirror was pale and blotchy, with black smudges from the eye make-up I hadn't taken off. I tottered into the living room in my rumpled, grubby, just-out-of-bed state, and found my mother reclining on the chaise longue in an apple-green silk kimono, fair hair piled high and gleaming, cheeks rosy, eyes bright. I was not looking forward to this meeting; particularly as I had a guilty feeling that Alex and I had probably made quite a lot of noise on our return to the building. Also, I'd left quite a few of her clothes flung about the place in my mad rush to find something to wear. However, her blue eyes were neither pooling with tears nor blazing with rage. In fact, she looked delighted to see me, almost as if we hadn't seen each other for days. 'Darling! Did you have a good time last night?'

'Er, yes,' I said, rather taken aback. 'Look, I'm sorry if—'

'Sorry? What have you got to be sorry about, you lucky girl?' She put down the scripts she had been reading and waved a manicured hand towards a magazine on the table. 'You know, now that you're older you're becoming really quite photogenic. Oh, darling, I'm so *proud.*' Dazed, I picked up the magazine and saw that it was the latest *Prattler,* open on a double-page spread of 'Miss India Withers's Sixteenth-Birthday Bash'. There we both were: 'Mr Alexis Withers and Miss Octavia Clairbrook-Cleeve.' We were standing very close, Alex was turned to me half smiling, but I had one hand slightly raised, as if to ward off the camera. I remembered the brightness of the flash, and how when I saw Alex through the dazzle it had felt like an omen. In the photo I looked rather cool and aloof, unsmiling, with that blocking hand. Eyes very black, face very pale, silk camisole half slipping off my shoulder. And Alex, turned to look at me, dark hair falling over his eyes, and his beautiful curling mouth . . .

I read on.

You would expect the daughter of rock royalty Rich Withers and ex-supermodel Tigerlily Clements to know how to throw one hell of a party – and this was an event that lived up to the highest expectations. Its 'white' theme may have been a cheeky nod to the Spilt Milk *spirit, but the emphasis here was firmly on the feminine and fantastical. Drifts of snow, flickering fairy lights and bowers of white roses added a touch of old-fashioned romance to an up-to-the-minute occasion. Music was provided by hot new band,* Purgatory, *and dress-down chic was the order of the day. India, a slim, vivacious blonde [pictured centre], looked stunning in a Zoë McCarthy ensemble especially created for the occasion. Champagne, candyfloss, vanilla ice cream and vodka cocktails kept energy levels high as the next generation of Beautiful People partied the night away . . .*

On the next page was a photo of Prince Richard, looking slightly bored and surrounded by four girls with extremely short skirts and fixed smiles. There was a picture of Asia (eyes closed and mouth open – not a good look) and one of the ice-angel and a few other shots of people I didn't recognize.

'Isn't it super?' My mother was bubbling over with excitement. 'Your photo is *right next* to the one of Prince Richard! Now,' she said coyly, 'is it just me, or does Alexis have his father's eyes? He *was* the chap I saw getting out of the cab last night, wasn't he?' My heart sank. I had had a nasty feeling that we'd made too much noise to escape undetected. 'I mean, I'd hate you to think I was prying. It's just, well, I'm such a light sleeper and the downstairs door makes *so* much noise and my window does face on to the street, you know . . . Oh, sweetheart! How exciting! I *knew* it would be all right!' She held up a hand-mirror and inspected her perfectly plucked eyebrows. 'You know that Rich and Tigerlily used to own the house just a bit along from us? The big Regency one with the columns? They moved out only couple of a months before we got this place . . . isn't it funny to think of you and India and Alexis almost being neighbours!'

'Nothing's happened, not really,' I muttered. 'I've only just met Alex . . . I don't know him that well.'

'Of course, of course. I do understand. Completely. These things are always so *delicate*.' She squeezed my hand fondly, then got up and started clearing things away in a brisk and business-like fashion. Watching her bustle around made me feel tired and slightly depressed. I had a sudden urge to sit her down again and tell her everything – about all the cocktails and LeeLee and the scary bouncers at the club. And Alex, standing in the middle of our street, so desirable, so effortlessly assured. *You're sweet . . .*

I sighed and rubbed my forehead, trying to massage away the faint throbbing sensation above my eyes. 'You don't think Alex is maybe too, um, old for me?'

She stopped what she was doing and turned to look at me. '*Nonsense*, Octavia. As long as you both like each other, that's all that matters and you shouldn't let anything else get in the way. You *do* like him, don't you?'

I looked over at the lovely glossy photo of the two of us. 'Of course.'

'Then where's the problem, you silly girl? This is a *very exciting* time for you and I think you should make the most of it. This is your *chance*.' Chance? For what? True love and turtle doves? Or my very own centre-page spread in the *Prattler*? But my mother had already moved on. 'And now, my darling, you'll have to get dressed. Make an effort, please, we're going to see your grandfather for lunch.'

I stared at her in horror. 'Oh no. Not today, I can't, *please.*'

'Don't be silly, Octavia. You haven't been for ages. And he so loves seeing you.'

This is blatantly untrue. My only surviving grandparent is not a cuddly old man who doles out toffees and sends funny packages through the post, or takes one out to tea and tells quaint stories about his youth. He is a nasty old git, as Michael once put it. When Dad finished university and announced that he was giving up law for the theatre my grandfather cut him off without a penny. When Dad left my mother (who my grand-father refused to meet) for another man, he declared that Hector was no son of his, that he had debased the noble name of the Clairbrook-Cleeves and that he never wanted to see or speak to him again. He thinks my mother is a vulgar gold-digger who somehow drove Dad into the arms of his own sex. He tolerates me as the Last in Line but sighs regretfully, and repeatedly, about how much he longs for a grandson. He could give India a run for her money when it comes to backhanded compliments and snide comments.

And yet to hear my mother talk about her father-in-law you'd think he was just a harmless eccentric, a lovable crank. 'Lord Clairbrook-Cleeve's always been *tricky*, of course, but he does *dote* on Octavia.' So about once a month we traipse out to his big gloomy house in Mayfair for lunch or coffee or whatever while he snipes at my mother and asks me torturous questions about what he calls my 'academic career'. Why my mother puts herself through this charade of dutiful-daughter-in-lawness is a mystery to me. She just sits through it all with this Glorious Martyr look on her face, like she's auditioning for Joan of Arc or something. You can practically smell the burning stake. As for me, it's quite a struggle to be docile and charming even when I'm at my bright-eyed best without a care in the world. In my current tetchy, tired and dehydrated state, this kind of performance would require nothing less than a miracle.

'Ah, little Octavia!' My grandfather met us at the door with his usual greeting, black eyes glinting with irony. If it wasn't for those cold, sharp eyes he would look like the perfect Nice Old Gentleman with his kindly, dignified face, his beautiful silver hair and aristocratically arched nose. 'Dear me! Have you grown some more since I saw you last? No? You know, Helen,' he said turning to my mother (he refuses to acknowledge that all-transforming 'a'), 'you really should stop giving the girl those American ready-meals. I've heard they put all sorts of steroids in them.' My grandfather likes to attribute all the world's evils, imaginary or not, to America. Or the north of England. 'Come in, come in. I do hope you're not still on one of your dieting fads, are you, Helen? Marie has spent all morning preparing a very special luncheon for you both.'

'I always look forward to Marie's cooking.' My mother's smile was fixed and glassy. Marie, the housekeeper, waits on my grandfather with a stony-faced devotion. When I'm not hung-over, I quite like her meals – traditional English stodge – but I could see her watching my mother slog through each calorific course with a triumphal sort of air (my grandfather merely toyed elegantly with a little clear soup). We ate in the dining room, which, like the rest of the house, is crowded with heirlooms of the Clairbrook-Cleeves: cloudy silver, misty mirrors, murky oils. Both my mother and I were somewhat pale by the end of the meal – I was desperately trying not to think of last night's purple cocktails churning around with the sherry trifle – but my grandfather was merciless.

'Now I *insist* you try some of this Stilton, Helen. I ordered it from Fortnum's especially. And Octavia, my dear, you're looking rather wan. I trust you're not ill? Perhaps you had something last night that did not agree with you?' He looked at me with a tender concern that didn't fool me for a minute.

We moved to the drawing room for coffee. His Lordship sank into the only comfortable chair in the room with a happy sigh. 'And now you must both bring me up to date with all your news. Tell me, Helen, are you still enjoying life in television advertising? Aren't you entertaining us all as a dancing yogurt pot?' This was a reference to a TV commercial my mother was in nearly ten years ago but which he still asks about as if it were an ongoing event. Then it was my turn. 'Octavia, I see, is making her society debut. Wining and dining with rock stars and royalty! Rubbing shoulders with heirs and graces!' He chuckled, practically rubbing his hands with relish. To my surprise, the satisfaction seemed genuine. But how on earth did he know about India's party? He answered this himself. 'Oh yes, I have my sources! I happen to be on the board of one of these fashionable charities – so tedious, but it is Expected of One – and they were holding a fund-raising ball or some such nonsense, which, of course, I absolutely *refused* to attend. But my dear old friend the Duchess of Teasedale sent me a copy of some silly magazine that covered the event, and then who did I spy with my little eye? My own granddaughter! *Such* a delightful surprise.'

He was genuinely pleased. Not that my grandfather would actually like or approve of India and Co., but he still respected what they *meant*. Wealth and glamour and influence. He and my mother were, for once, in perfect harmony – overjoyed that I was cosying up to the big-of-name, large-of-fortune and small-of-brain. However, the *Prattler* article at least spared me the usual cross-examination on the failings of the modern secondary education system in general and my own eccentric education in particular. Instead, my grandfather took the photo of Prince Richard as his inspiration for a lecture on the British class system ('I'm sure that you, Helen, with your proletarian roots, can appreciate the traditional affection felt by the working class towards our royals . . .'). All in all, I felt I'd got off pretty lightly, but both my mother and I let out sighs of relief once we had said our goodbyes and Marie had shut the door behind us with a satisfied slam.

'Yet another joyous family love-fest with Grandpa Cleeve. Don't you just feel all warm and gooey inside?' I finally said once we were in the car and safely away. My mother didn't comment. She never does, just goes tight-lipped and noble looking, like she does around Dad. This makes me feel guilty, and also annoyed.

'Well?'

'Well what?'

'Well, he's awful, isn't he?'

'He's your only surviving grandparent and an old man,' said St Joan, with a gentle yet pained smile. 'We must do our duty and be patient, darling.'

'I bet Attila the Hun was somebody's grandpa. Doesn't mean he wasn't a murdering maniac.'

'Lord Clairbrook-Cleeve may be a Tory peer but he is hardly a murdering maniac.'

'Pity. Else he'd probably be locked up by now.' I tried another argument. 'I just don't see why we have to suck up to him like this. It's not like we're ever going to *get* anything out of him.' His Lordship has, indeed, signed away most of his loot to Ye League For Ye Protection Of Olde Englysh Values. Or something.

'*Octavia*. That is an appalling thing to say!'

'But then again the family silver's probably cursed. Ill-gotten gains and all that. A bit of ancestral rape and pillage—'

'I won't hear any more of this. You're being ridiculous and offensive.'

'I must take after my grandfather, then.'

We spent the rest of the drive in frosty silence. However, as we pulled up to the last traffic lights before home she suddenly said, 'Do you remember your other grandparents – my parents, I mean?'

'Not much,' I said cautiously. My mother didn't have much to do with her parents after fleeing the north of England for her career as America's favourite English Rose. From something Dad had once said, I gathered that her parents hadn't exactly kept the home fires burning on her account. They both died some years ago, but I do just remember being taken to Newcastle to visit them when I was little. Their terraced house was dark and narrow; it was a very hot day, and there was a stale sort of Sunday-lunch smell in the hall. We sat in a very small, very neat front room, and though I don't remember much else about the visit I remember how the Sunday-lunch smell was mixed up in my mind with a looming sense of disapproval. My mother was wearing a short skirt that she kept tugging at so that it covered her knees, and I remember her talking on and on in a light, quick, nervous voice that eventually trailed off into silence. But of course I didn't mention all this.

'No, I suppose you wouldn't.' She sighed, and

looked a bit sad. I wanted to say something, to make it right, but I wasn't quite sure what was wrong. And with her next remark it was right back to the reading-from-different-scripts again. 'You know,' she said brightly, 'you really should have India round one evening after school. I mean, if you carry on seeing Alexis, she'll almost be like a sister, won't she?'

My almost-sister cornered me in the girls' toilets on Monday lunchtime. Asia, Calypso and China were in tow, Asia shooting me evil looks in between each application of mascara. This time the catchphrase on her sherbet-pink T-shirt was PSYCHO BITCH, embroidered in red hearts. I found it hard to believe that she wore it in a spirit of light-hearted irony. India's outfit was not quite so scary – a cream satin corset, skin-tight jeans and a long, tattered sheepskin coat – but she was playing with her charm bracelet in a menacing sort of way.

'Hello, Obelisk,' said India pleasantly. 'Did you enjoy Friday night?'

'Yes, thanks,' I said warily.

'And did my naughty brother try to take advantage of you?' The others giggled. But although India's tone was playful she was watching me narrowly. So Alex didn't tell her everything. This was a relief, but I wasn't sure how to answer the question – if I said no, it would be like admitting I wasn't worth the effort of seducing and India would look surprised, pitying and smug in turn. If I said yes . . . well, there would be more cross-examination, innuendo and exaggeration, and whatever version of events I came up with would doubtless be relayed to Alex with God-knows-what variations.

I found myself blushing but managed to say lightly, 'Well, you know what they say: "nice girls may kiss but they never tell."' This was dangerous ground; only last year, India's mother had serialized her autobiography – complete with lurid details of her ex-husband's sex life – in one of the tabloids. However, India merely shrugged and turned to fluff up her hair in the mirror; I even thought there was a momentary, if grudging, glint of respect in her eyes.

I began to sidle out, but before I got to the door she turned to me again. 'I just *adore* LeeLee, don't you?'

'She was . . . nice, yeah.'

'She used to go out with Lex. I'm sure he told you, of course . . . they've always got on *so* well. So much in common. She's a model, you know.' Great. 'And she's been like a sister to me.' Oh fantastic. 'But,' said India, sweet as pie, '*but* I have been telling Lex *how well* the two of us get on. How much fun you are.' I stared at her. 'Lex always sets such store by his baby sister's opinion. It's quite touching, really . . .' She trailed off dreamily. Then she shook out her hair, briskly straightened her coat, and picked up her bag as if to leave. 'Oooh yes. I nearly forgot. In a couple of weeks' time – on the Friday – we've got "Take Your Daughter to Work Day", haven't we?' It was news to me that Darlinham House paid any attention to this particular government initiative, but then our school always seized on any excuse to give everyone the day off. The school even shut down in honour of National Incontinence Awareness Day. I had an uncomfortable suspicion, however, where this particular train of thought was leading. 'Poor old Dad's in his Buddhist monastery all week, so that's no go. But I was thinking, wouldn't it be fun if I came along with you instead . . . paid a visit to your father on his film set, I mean. I feel that we *really connected* that time we met.' I cleared my throat. '*Do* say yes. I've been going on about it to Lex *all weekend*. And you know how much he looks out for me.'

Our eyes met. Here was my chance to make a stand, to show India once and for all that I was not the sort of girl who allowed herself to be pushed around by a spoilt blonde dwarf with a superiority complex. What sort of pathetic, desperate loser would grovel after the most loathsome girl in the school just so they could cop off with her brother? So what if this brother was heart-breakingly handsome and over six-foot tall? The real issue here was one of personal integrity and self-respect and I knew exactly what I should do. I took a deep breath. 'I'll have to speak to Dad first,' I heard myself saying, 'but that's fine. I'm sure that'll be fine.'

After India and the rest had gone a horrible thought occurred to me. Never mind the principles I'd just trampled over in my slobbering rush for romantic fulfilment – had India *deliberately* set me up with Alex so she'd be extra sure of access to Drake and Oscar nominations? I went hot and cold at the idea, but then I remembered her at the bar on Friday and how when she caught my eye she had the look of someone who's just had an unpleasant surprise. I couldn't really believe that Alex would go to the bother of chasing a girl he wasn't interested in just to please his sister, but still . . . I kicked at the wall with frustration.

It was only when I leaned down to rub my stubbed toe that I realized Jess was standing behind me. She must have heard India and her posse on their way out.

'Lex?' she asked, staring. 'You're going out with Lex, as in India's *brother*?'

'Not "going out", exactly. I pulled him at the party, sort of by accident, before I knew who he was. I didn't think anything would come of it, but then he phoned on Friday. And we went out with lots of other people, India included.' I said this a bit awkwardly, thinking that maybe I should have told her about this in the beginning. I was half afraid that Jess would look at me with disgust or, at the very least, total incredulity. But she didn't – in fact she seemed pleased.

'Good for you! India must be seething.'

'Yeah, in fact she's so mad she's behaving like she's my new best friend and is gushing to Alex about how cool I am,' I said in doom-laden tones.

'She is? Why?'

'Blackmail. The not-so-subtle message behind our little chat just now was that if I don't play along with her plans to ambush Drake Montague . . . well, my first date with Alex will definitely be my last.'

'Does she really have that much influence over him? She's probably just winding you up, we never heard much about her precious Lex until last week or so.'

'Maybe. They seemed pretty cosy on Friday night.'

Jess looked at me curiously. 'Isn't Alex . . . well, isn't it a bit like dating India?'

I shrugged. 'I don't know, to be honest. I don't *think* so. But I want to find out for myself, in my own time, in my own way. Not with his "baby sister" breathing down both our necks.' I still couldn't believe I'd caved in to India like that – what was I thinking? But I wasn't thinking, that was the problem. I was lusting. 'Oh, *God*, why the hell couldn't Alex have been an only child? What on earth am I going to say to Dad? And what will I *do* with her, *say* to her, that Friday?' A sudden thought occurred to me. 'I don't suppose you'd like to come, would you? We could go off and do our own thing and leave India to it. I just don't think I can face it on my own.'

Jess tucked a stray red curl behind her ear. 'Well, I suppose,' she said calmly. She paused for thought. 'India might not be very pleased . . .' she smiled her slow, quiet smile '. . . and that's a good enough reason for me.'

In my defence, I hadn't surrendered to India's latest campaign for world domination simply because a few Alex-obsessed hormones told me to. OK, so he was the first eligible male I'd practically ever met and the fantastic, unbelievable fact that he'd shown any interest in me at all was enough to make me feel goddess- rather than obelisk-like. But Alex or no Alex, any fool knew that to stand between India and something she wanted was reckless to the point of suicidal.

Take Mr Marti Craddock, for example. Mr Craddock was a one-time minor singing sensation who'd had a couple of top-ten hits in the late eighties. When musical tastes had moved on he somehow ended up as the biology teacher at Darlinham House where, as well as teaching the birds and the bees to a load of jaded Darlings, he was also our Head of Year. Unfortunately for him, Mr Craddock took pastoral care a bit more seriously than the rest of the staff. Even more unfortunately, it was while we were under his paternal eye that little Indy embarked on a romance with one of the school's security guards, a former stuntman who claimed to be on first-name terms with every action hero worth his baby-oiled pecs. And most unfortunate of all, when Mr Craddock caught them snogging behind the weight-lifting machine in the fitness suite he wrote a note to India's papa, warning him of this 'undesirable association'. God knows what Rich Withers thought about it, but in the end it couldn't have mattered much as Mr Muscles was swiftly dumped both by India and the school after it was discovered that his stuntman heroics were as bogus as his security qualifications. However, Mr Craddock's fate was already sealed.

Mr Craddock, we were informed, was leaving Darlinham House to relaunch his singing career. His old record company had taken him up again and it was announced that he was shortly to release his comeback single, a syrupy ballad to the joys of fatherhood called 'Baby Lovin''. In order to wish him luck for his new venture and to show our year's appreciation for all he had done for us, India invited him to stop by at a little class party she was throwing to mark the end of term. Ever since the security-guard episode India had been sweetness and light towards him – which a wiser man than Marti would have realized meant Serious Trouble. Sure enough, Mr Craddock duly turned up to say his goodbyes only to find that India had neglected to tell him that her end-of-term party had a 'St Trinian's' theme. No boys had been invited, but Asia and China and Calypso and the rest of the pygmy blondes were there, together with quite a few girls from the lower years, all dressed in naughty schoolgirl outfits. Slightly nonplussed, Mr

Craddock soon made his excuses and left, but not before he'd been persuaded to pose with them all for 'one last photo to remember you by, sir'!

Of course, it didn't take long for a copy of this photo to find its way both to his record company and the school notice board. You can imagine how it looked – a grown man (a *teacher* no less!) romping around with a horde of skimpily dressed under-age schoolgirls . . . Presumably Mr Craddock's explanations were enough to prevent an official inquiry, but that was the end of 'Baby Lovin'' and his comeback tour.

Admittedly, this was an extreme example of what happens to those who try to thwart India Withers. I could, however, think of plenty of other incidents to send a chill down my spine. Like Desdemona Hughes, who once had the nerve to assert – in mixed company – that India's new leather trousers did not, perhaps, display her peach-like bottom to its best possible advantage. Once again, photographic technology was the weapon of choice. This time India got hold of a photo of her victim that China, whose mother is the fashion editor of *Venus* magazine, digitally enhanced so that Dezzie's own posterior ballooned to epic proportions. The next week, this image adorned posters advertising 'Instant Arse Reduction – Miracle Cure!!!' that had mysteriously appeared on every lamp-post and billboard within a three-mile radius of Darlinham House. Below the photo was a number for the telephone helpline. It only took fifteen phone calls asking for 'Lard-Arse Solutions' before Dezzie fled both her mobile and the school in tears, never to return.

Then there was Isaiah Chadwick-Templeton, a

super-stud from the year above who was reckless enough to remark that India kissed like a T-rex on heat. The next morning a cleaner found him passed out in the care-taker's cupboard, wearing nothing but a lacy pink thong, fishnet stockings and heels. Darlinham House being Darlinham House, there was no investigation and no question of him being expelled, but ever since the pink-thong incident Isaiah has been a shadow of his former self.

I was made of sterner stuff than Dezzie, I couldn't be seduced like Isaiah and I didn't have a comeback to launch or a record to sell, like Mr Craddock. I could even think of worse things than being hounded out of Darlinham House. But I did want Alex and I did want a quiet life. So, as much as I hated the idea, it made a lot of sense to go along with India's sordid little schemes.

When I got home a package had arrived for me from Alex. Inside the box was a tiny white rose made of spun sugar with green marzipan leaves. The hastily scrawled note read, *Here's to moonlit memories of Octavia! Some friends of mine in a band have got a gig this Wednesday – you should come along??? X.* I'd be lying if I said I didn't go all girly and blushful when I saw the rose, even though it occurred to me that it was probably a leftover from India's birthday celebrations.

I showed my trophies to Viv, who had come round for the evening, supposedly to compare notes on *Macbeth*. (Although educational qualifications are not top priority for most Darlings, our school fees have to be justified by a veneer of academic respectability.

Sometimes we're even set an essay deadline or two.) Of course, the moment Viv and I shut ourselves in my room we abandoned all thought of coursework preparation and settled down to paint our toenails and flick through my mother's old magazines. And gossip, naturally.

I hadn't wanted to tell her about Friday night over the phone, so it was a luxury to talk face to face with someone who didn't know anyone involved, didn't have any ulterior motive and who would see things exactly from my point of view. Not that Viv was bursting with enthusiasm.

'So Prince Charming's got a bit of a reputation, right? And his ugly sister's using him to pull your strings? And you're still going to play along?'

I rolled over on to my back and examined the ceiling. It was different for Viv; boys fell for her all the time and even though she might shrug off her fan club with a dismissive smile . . . well, this was a new experience for me. Because although I didn't feel entirely at ease with Alex, was out of my depth even, it still felt good to be wanted by him. To see girls like WeeWee sulking as he put his arm round me. To have his mates eyeing me admiringly. To feel as if my midriff was melting every time he kissed me. To be sent white sugar roses through the post, like a proper romantic heroine.

I tried to explain some of this to Viv, but it all came out like a particularly syrupy extract from *Tammy Gets Kissed*. She still didn't look entirely convinced. 'No offence, Octavia, but it's not as if you've got much to compare Alex with. I'm sure he's a big improvement on Zip or Zap or whoever, but is that going to be enough?'

'I do have some standards, you know,' I said, irritated. 'You can't pass through puberty in the company of Darlings and stay naive for very long. I could probably tell you more about over-privileged, over-rated and over-sexed males than *Spilt Milk's* biographer.' I was also thinking about the Tammy book again. Tammy got tangled up with a handsome seducing type (captain of the school football team, as I recall), but when it all went amiss she fell into the arms of her best male friend, a funny, dependable, sensitive-yet-manly type who'd been pining for her secretly all the time. My closest equivalent to this was, er, Zack. But I wasn't under the same illusions as Tammy and I would therefore be careful around Alex. I would be friendly but nonchalant, alluring but just a little aloof.

'I've not gone soft in the head,' I said. 'I know Alex probably isn't going to turn out to be my knight in shining armour. I'm not in love with him – but I do *like* him, and I think he likes me back. It's a good feeling.' I paused for thought, working things out as I went along. 'For the first time since I got dumped in that horrible school I feel as if I could be . . . part of things, but – and this is the good bit – in a highly selective, non-painful, part-time sort of way. I know it's going to be tricky, getting round India and everything, but can't you see how much easier life would be if this works out?'

Viv raised her brows. 'So whatever happened to living life as Ms Normal?'

'*Normal* people go to parties and have boyfriends and spend their schooldays with people who actually know their name. I don't see why I have to be the exception for the rest of my miserable teenage life . . . Look, all I'm saying is that if I make a go of it with Alex I'll be able to hold my head up at school, I become the daughter of my mother's dreams *and* I get to be with a fun, sexy guy who's got a thing for Godzilla-sized brunettes.'

'I see. The have-your-cake-and-eat-it philosophy.'

'Philosophy? It's our school motto.'

'OK, OK,' said Viv. 'Maybe you're right and you do know what you're doing. But I still don't see the problem with India going to the film set and meeting Drake. He's probably just as awful as she is. So what if she seduces him and goes to Hollywood? At least she can't seduce your *father.*'

I shuddered. 'No, thank God. But you should have seen her with Dad at the party . . . all starry-eyed and oozing sincerity. Because the awful thing is, she really *can* act. And she's no dumb blonde. She's smart. Really smart – she had all the right ideas about Dad's last play, she was talking about things I'd never even heard of. So she probably will worm her way into his good books, and once she turns on the charm with Drake there'll be no stopping her. She'll be everywhere I go, with everyone I've ever known . . .'

'You're starting to sound really paranoid.' Viv examined her newly painted big toe. 'You're *both* weird. I mean, why should India care about you snogging her brother?'

'Because India's written me off as D-list. I'm not fun or glamorous or well-connected, at least not in her terms. The Obelisk, remember. It's a personal affront to have her precious brother lowering family standards to pay attention to me. As far as she's concerned, anyone with any connection to her should be *way* out of my league.'

'Leagues? Listings? D grades? This is boy-meets-girl, not an Ofsted inspection.'

'Little do you know. Look.' I tossed over an old copy of *Prattler.*

' "Beautiful People: The Next Generation," ' Viv read aloud. Inside the magazine was a list of twenty 'names to look out for' with accompanying pictures of the tarted-up children of aristocrats and celebrities.

'India and Alex are both there,' I explained. 'India's the youngest person on the list. They say that Alex is already set to become "one of our most eligible bachelors". It's absolute crap, of course, just sucking up to their readership. You only buy this sort of magazine if you and your friends are in it. But India and Co. take this sort of thing very, very seriously.' As does my mother, I added silently. I suspected that it was no accident that this particular copy of the magazine had been left lying out for me to find.

Viv snorted, but didn't say anything for a while, leafing through the *Prattler* and last month's *Venus* magazine. 'OK, Octavia, I've found the solution to all your problems.' It was an article entitled 'Ten Tricks to Tame a Bad Boy'. There was a picture of a very glamorous girl in red leather, brandishing a whip. I looked at her voluptuous WeeWee-type pout and even more voluptuous breasts and sighed.

'Should post-feminists read glossy magazines?'

'The jury's still out,' said Viv cheerfully. 'Personally, I think they're pornography for women. Sordid, exploitative . . . only momentarily satisfying . . . but

FUN. Listen, it says here that "all bad boys love the thrill of the chase. So once he's hunted you down, keep him guessing. Be mysterious and secretive. If need be, hint at a shadowy past." ' She hunched over, narrowed her eyes and lowered her voice to a throaty whisper. 'Alas, I cannot possibly join you at the Rah Bar tonight. There are people after me. The Dark Side's agents are closing in. I have very little time. How about chips from the kebab van instead?' We started laughing and once we'd started we couldn't stop, until at last Lady J. rapped on the door to tell us to shut up and get some work done. So what with the giggling and then *Macbeth* I didn't think about Alex/India/Drake for the rest of the evening.

'Dad?'

'Octavia! I'm so glad – I was just saying to Michael that it was time to give you a ring. We haven't yet congratulated you on your guest appearance.'

'Guest appearance?'

'Yes! Amidst the glossy pages of the bitchy and shameless.' (This is an old joke between us, our own private rhyming slang for the rich and famous.)

'Oh . . . right. Thanks.'

'Your mother must be very pleased.'

'Ecstatic. Listen, Dad, how's the filming going?'

'Not too bad, actually. I thought there might be problems with having a megastar on set, but Drake seems strangely keen on making himself agreeable. Most peculiar.'

'Um, I don't suppose I could come along sometime and see you in action?' And, er, maybe bring some friends?'

There was a pause.

'Look, Octavia, you know the way I like to work – absolute concentration and no distractions. A film set's not for tourists, and what with the Drake effect it's going to be tricky getting clear of journalists and auto- graph hunters and so on. I don't mind if it's just you but . . .'

'Dad, I don't like to pester, and I wouldn't norm- ally, but we really wouldn't be any trouble.' I wasn't entirely sure of this, but never mind. 'It's for a school project – a national, *government* one, actually – "Take Your Daughter to Work Day". Equal opportunities and all that.'

'Most commendable, but the last time I checked I only had the one.'

'One what?'

'Daughter. According to my calculations that would be you – unless there's something your mother hasn't been telling me?'

'Yes. No, I mean, but . . . Look – I don't want to bring a *crowd*. It's just me and Jess, you know, who you met at Speech Day and . . . and . . .' I couldn't quite bring myself to say the next word.

'And?'

'India.'

'Ah. The one who gave the party?'

'Yes.'

'I remember India. Cold steel and candyfloss, as you put it . . . hmm.' Pause. Then, shrewdly, 'It was her brother who was in that photograph with you, wasn't it?' I found myself blushing down the other end of the phone.

'Yes. Alex.'

'I see. When do you want this jaunt of yours? When Drake's around, I suppose?'

'The Friday after next, if that's OK. Oh, Dad—'

'Never mind the "oh, Dad" bit. You can come. All of you. But I will hold you personally responsible if there are any interruptions, any distractions, and I mean *any*, to hold things up on set.'

'Thanks, this is so great, I really, really—'

'I just hope he's worth it.'

In spite of all my brave words to Viv, I found myself hoping the same thing on Wednesday evening while I was waiting for Alex to pick me up, skulking in my room to avoid my mother. Not that she objected to me going out late on a school night – oh no, if the son of Rich Withers was involved, who was she to stand in the way of true romance and maybe even a gossip-column byline? However, I knew that once she started looking me over with a critical eye and making helpful 'suggestions' as to my appearance, I would spend the whole night in a state of body dysmorphic paranoia. She'd already stopped me eating pasta for supper – 'carbohydrates are so *bloating*, Octavia' – and told me off for wearing chipped nail polish. I remembered how great she'd been about India's party, with the shopping trips and everything, and how I'd actually enjoyed doing all that stuff with her. But ever since then she hadn't stopped fussing about my hair, my clothes, my make-up . . . even the way I put on a coat and walked into a room. She clearly didn't believe that my inherently lovable personality and sparkling conversational skills were enough to get me my man. The problem was, neither did I.

Alex was fifteen minutes late and arrived in a taxi, rather than roaring up in the big black convertible I had secretly pictured. He was looking rather rumpled, with tousled hair and wearing an old T-shirt and jeans. As he leaned forward to talk to the driver I looked at his dark hair curling into the back of his smooth brown neck and felt a lurch of longing. During the taxi ride we joked and chatted together as he played with my hand and told me the story of this band, Knife, that we were going to hear and how they were all set to be the Next Big Thing. 'When, of course, everyone else will like and start talking about them,' he said with one of his sleepy smiles, 'so there won't be any point in going to see them. You're only just in time.'

Knife were apparently about to be signed by Brimstone Records, the ultra-hip independent music label where Alex was doing his internship. 'It's real hands-on stuff, very intense, but it's cool to be part of the creative process, you know?' He told me he was still undecided as to whether he should take up his place to read media studies at university next year or go straight into the music business. 'I want to work from the inside, be the man who discovers the talent and pulls the strings . . . and everyone knows the kind of abilities you need for that can't be taught or certified on some diploma. Picking a winner should be instinctive but it's also about *connecting*. You have to tap into the zeitgeist, keep your ear to the ground, your finger on the pulse . . .' I nodded solemnly, even though the latter requirements sounded more like a yoga position than a career strategy. I'm not sure my earnest air fooled him, how-ever, because he looked at me sidelong and grinned. 'God, listen to me drone on. Just shut me up if you hear me getting pompous, will you? Indy says I'm turning into a music bore.'

'Pompous, maybe. But boring? Never!' I said as we clambered out of the cab. Alex looked a bit taken aback, then took a pretend swipe at my head.

'Don't be cheeky. Everybody knows I'm really a model of humility.'

I swiped him back. 'Glad to hear it, Mr Modesty.'

The gig was in a deconsecrated church in South London with a big neoclassical portico and columns. The columns were cracked and there were heaps of rubble outside, but all this added to rather than detracted from its air of seedy, slightly sinister grandeur. Lurid blue lighting burned from within. 'All very apocalyptic,' I said, impressed. Alex, however, assumed I was being disparaging.

'Oh, God, I know. *So* pre-millennium. But at least with a place like this the acoustics are bound to be good.'

The band had already started when we pushed our way into the thick of the crowd. Most people there appeared to know Alex and there was much slapping on the back and raising of hands in greeting, but the music was much too loud for any attempts at conversation. In fact, the music was almost too loud to hear what the band was actually playing, if you see what I mean. I could feel the noise shudder in my ribcage; my ears and brain seemed to be quaking and ringing with the assault. It made me feel a bit sick after a while.

Nonetheless, I smiled and nodded my head along with the rest of them, and when the band took a break I tried to join in the energetic babble of acclaim and criticism around me. Viv and I bounce around to whatever's at the top of the charts at the moment, otherwise I like listening to some of the classical stuff Dad's into, so I couldn't really contribute to the analysis of 'synthesizer scribbles' and 'single-bar dropouts' and 'punk-funk bass' the others were discussing. However, Alex was flushed and bright-eyed and talking eagerly – it was the most animated I had ever seen him.

I suppose it was only to be expected, considering his background, but I found this new, enthusiastic Alex surprising and rather endearing. It occurred to me that his more usual air of fashionable detachment might only be skin-deep. I didn't have much time to ponder this before the band started again, but once I'd got used to the noise level I almost began to enjoy myself. The people were more relaxed and a lot less polished-looking than those at the Rah Bar, everyone got a bit sweaty and dishevelled, and when the set was finished, with one last crash and a shuddering wail, we all surged forward excitedly. The band had been playing on a raised platform where the altar had once been, and once they'd finished they immediately scrambled down and joined their friends in the crowd; the lead singer and the bass guitarist both came up to Alex amid even more back-slapping and banter. 'Who's the latest?' asked the singer finally, jerking his head towards me.

'Jools, Octavia. Octavia, Jools,' said Alex, and immediately plunged back into a highly technical discussion about buzz-saw guitar riffs. I didn't think much of Jools

– his small pale eyes reminded me of Zack and his exaggeratedly cockney accent occasionally slipped into something more at home in Sloane Square. However, now that the music had stopped and the church was a bit less crowded, I managed to have more of a conversation with the people we'd been standing with and soon found myself chatting away to the bass guitarist. I was worried about saying something that would expose my ignorance of electro clash and the rest of it but he was a big, relaxed guy with a mop of sweaty fair hair and a cheerful grin.

'Actually, I quite like a bit of classical music myself,' he told me.

'Really?'

'Yeah. Beethoven's Ninth, for example. Now that's got a pumping bass line.'

For a moment I thought he was serious, then I caught the twinkle in his eye. 'Absolutely. And I've always admired Brahms for his fusion of trip hop with acid blues – so ahead of his time.'

'Subverted by Chopin, of course, with his impromptu use of thrash garage.'

We were laughing at this when Alex came up and took my arm, a bit possessively, I thought. 'The after-gig party is going on at Jools's place. You ready to go?' Most people were leaving the church by now, so we stepped back into a corner to avoid getting caught up in the exodus.

'I'd actually rather not. It's been a really good night, but it's quite late and . . . and I have got school tomorrow,' I finished lamely. He didn't seem annoyed by this, but smiled and drew me closer.

'OK. How about a quiet night in with me instead? It's not even midnight. You could come back with me, we could have a drink, listen to some music and stuff, have some, you know, fun . . . Dad's in Tibet with his monks and Indy's God knows where, as usual. We'd have the place to ourselves.' His arm was firm around my waist and his lovely curling mouth warm and whispering against my ear. I looked over his head and saw Jools waiting outside. He was watching us and saying something to a friend. They were both smirking.

I drew away from Alex and avoided his eyes. 'Not tonight.'

He bent to kiss my neck. 'Where's the harm? You like me, don't you? I'd take good care of you, I promise.'

I managed to laugh even though my heart was pounding along to the cardiovascular equivalent of techno-thrash. 'That's very kind of you, but I can take good care of myself.'

'Which is why you won't come back with me?' Now he was annoyed, and there was a sneer in his voice. 'What's the matter, you afraid I won't "respect you in the morning"?'

I realized, with a cold, sinking feeling, that this was probably the end of Alex and me. Glowering, with his face flushed and hair rumpled, he looked even more sexy than usual – so what was *wrong* with me? I wasn't an ice-angel, I could melt into his arms and still be there in the morning . . . I knew WeeWee or Asia or Tallulah or any of the others wouldn't be dithering around like this – in fact, they'd probably be ravishing Alex behind a pillar by now. But Alex hadn't chosen to be with any of them tonight, I reminded myself. He'd chosen *me*.

And now I was going to make my own choice. I lifted my chin and looked him in the eye.

'Actually,' I said, as lightly as I could, 'that's not really the issue. It's a matter of whether *I* would respect me in the morning.' Viv would be proud, I thought, but not without a pang of regret.

Now, however, and somewhat to my surprise, he merely shrugged his shoulders. He had that amused, half-admiring, half-puzzled look he'd had when we first met. 'I can't work you out.'

'Well, that's hardly surprising. We barely know each other.'

'I thought I was proposing a way to get to know each other better.'

I gave him a look. 'If you want to get to know me *that* way, you'll have to get to know me *my* way first.'

'Your way?'

'Yeah. So far we've only seen each other in the middle of a crowd. OK, they're your friends and it's been fun. But next time,' I crossed my sweaty fingers behind my back, 'if you still want a next time, that is, I think just the two of us should go out somewhere.'

'Coffee and cake for two, you mean? Holding hands in a park? Feeding the birds? Sitting on a bench, watching the world go by?' His tone was mocking but he'd put his arm back around my waist and I took courage from it. I felt as if I'd just passed the first stage of a difficult test, and that maybe Alex had too. Not with flying colours, exactly, but it was a *start*.

'Come on, Alex, live a little. What's the matter, you too cool to be seen throwing bread to ducks? Or will you only commit to coffee with the girl you're planning to marry? Because I have to warn you – I'm not the marrying kind.'

He looked a bit sheepish. 'OK. So the two of us will go out on Saturday. That's a promise. Now, how about a compromise – come to this party with me . . . Please?'

It was past four when I let myself into the flat. 'Jools's place' was, as I'd suspected, a regency mansion in the slums of Chelsea, and it seemed that nearly everyone who'd been at the gig had made their way there. More gloomy, shrieking music was played and everybody smoked and drank a lot and had very long, very boring, very confused philosophical debates about existentialism and moral relativism. In spite of this, I was glad I went. The bass guitarist, whose name was Nick, found me again and was so chatty and attentive that Alex abandoned arguing for the impossibility of God in favour of coming up to us both, putting an assertive arm around my shoulder and scowling. I don't think it did any harm for Alex to see someone else paying me some attention, especially as WeeWee turned up towards the end of the night. But she and Jools disappeared together very soon after, so I felt able to say goodbye to Alex without fear of anyone seducing him in my absence. I was particularly cheered by his parting words. 'Sorry if I was, ah, less than the perfect gentleman tonight. I suppose I'm not used to . . . um . . .' He looked down rather shamefacedly. 'Sometimes I forget you're that bit younger and . . . well, you're different from the others anyway. Different in a *good* way, I mean. You won't hold tonight against me, will you?'

The next, or rather the same morning, I had good

reason to curse my new resolution to get up ten minutes early to allow for extra grooming. Although I hadn't been drinking, my head was ringing from battered eardrums and lack of sleep; we had double English first thing in the morning, which I'm usually quite good at, but barely got through without keeling over. India was too busy mentally rehearsing her Academy Award acceptance speech to pay me more attention than a chummily suggestive smile, which Asia and Zack, in celebration of their recent reunion, followed up with a series of suggestive and not particularly chummy sniggers.

Luckily for me, Darlinham House is not the sort of place to enforce student participation in class activities. Although we are supposedly on first-name terms with Opal, our English teacher, she is, like most of the staff there, known as 'Er . . .' to her face and 'What's-her-name' behind her back. She has bravely tried to resist this culture of anonymity by coming to lessons decked out in tropical-print turbans, sequinned boob tubes and multicoloured hair extensions, but the fact remains that ninety-five per cent of her students wouldn't recognize her if she ran them over in the street.

'So,' she began nervously, 'I really enjoyed reading your essays on *American Psycho* last week. Phoenix even illustrated his with diagrams showing exactly how each murder was committed! They were very, er, accomplished.' Glassy smile. 'Now, we've already had a little discussion about the similarities between *Macbeth* and *American Psycho*. Let's get back to Shakespeare's text. You've all read the play by now, so any thoughts?' She looked around her rather hopelessly. 'Did you love it?

Hate it? Is Shakespeare a better writer than Bret Easton Ellis? Worse?'

Silence, apart from the buzz of Ulysses's personal stereo, the rustling of India's magazine and the rasping of Calypso's nail file.

'Anyone?' The familiar note of desperation was already creeping into her voice. She took a deep breath. 'OK, maybe we should look at a specific aspect of the text. Let's just concentrate on the characters for now. What do you think about the character of Lady Macbeth?'

Long, long pause. Opal's nervous twitch had started up again.

Finally, 'Lady M. is the heroine of the play,' India announced graciously, then returned to her magazine. Opal had tears of gratitude in her eye.

'That's very *interesting*. A very *profound* observation. And as a matter of fact, quite a few critics have said—'

'*I* would say that it's all a matter of style.'

'Style of leadership? Is that what you mean, India?'

'Style *is* leadership,' put in Calypso, examining a freshly painted petrol-green talon.

'That's right!' Opal exclaimed. 'The cult of the personality! Charisma! And what happens when the Macbeths can no longer take refuge in their public persona?' Dramatic pause. 'The facade crumbles! Ruin! Madness! Death!'

'Yes, well. The public-relations industry has moved on a bit since then,' said India pityingly. Suddenly the rest of the class woke into life.

'Macbeth should have handled the Duncan-Banquo scandal through an official spokesperson.'

'Then the two of them could have concentrated on their image management, not just damage limitation.'

'Lady M. is a sort of Princess Di figure, don't you think? Only more evil.'

'Yeah, so why didn't they make the most of her breakdown? Macbeth didn't need to go into *details*, just, you know, go for the sympathy vote.'

'The trick is to give the public what they want to hear. You have to sound sincere even when you're holding stuff back . . . like those witches. If only Macbeth had got them onside . . .'

'Spin-witches for the House of Cawdor!' put in Opal merrily, caught up in the thrill of a real, live class discussion. There was an abrupt silence.

'Let's not go *overboard*,' said India crushingly, and everyone settled down to being terminally unresponsive again.

I wasn't in any of the same classes as Jess after lunch, which in the normal course of things would have meant a very dismal afternoon indeed. However, Tallulah – who had clearly revised her opinion of me after our little chat at the party – offered me a spritz of her cell-renewing skin tonic after Pilates, and Cosmo went so far as to ask my opinion in an extra-curricular debate on the merits of Russian versus Swedish vodka. The Alex effect, presumably. Either that or my extra primping time was already paying off.

I caught up with Jess in the school library. This is actually one of the nicer places in Darlinham House: a sunny room filled with big squishy sofas, where the *Encyclopaedia Britannica* fights a losing battle with stacks of glossy magazines and lifestyle journals. There's even a coffee bar, manned by a succession of haughty fashion students who have been known to kick people out if they spend too much time reading books and not buying lattes.

'Oh, hello,' said Jess, looking dreamily up at me from the magazine she'd been absorbed in. 'I've been doing some research.' It was a copy of *Venus* ('for your inner sex-goddess') and the cover squealed EXCLUSIVE DRAKE MONTAGUE INTERVIEW!!!! 'It's a back issue from when Drake was promoting *Psychlone* last summer,' she explained. 'Take a look . . . are you doing something different with your hair, by the way?'

'Er, yeah.' I patted it self-consciously. As I'd suspected, the sexily dishevelled look was a lot harder to pull off than the merely unkempt one, but I thought I'd better put in some practice before my next date with Alex.

'It looks nice.'

'Thanks.'

'I heard Seth telling Phoenix how he's always thought you had potential.' Jess looked wistful, and I suddenly felt embarrassed by my primping before the mirror.

'Potential for what? *Everyone's* got potential – we all know Phoenix is a potential axe murderer, for example. And Seth is a just a dirty old man in the making. Give us a look at the magazine, then, and let's see what we're in for.'

The interview was clearly intended for girls who drool themselves to sleep every night at the thought of Mr Montague, so the magazine had kindly provided them with a pull-out poster of Drake pouting on a beach. He was wearing a T-shirt that clung to every perfectly defined muscle on his chest, and his sun-streaked hair tumbled over moody grey eyes. They stared out of the page in a vacant sort of way. His chiselled jaw was clenched in a manner meant to suggest manly fortitude, but actually put me in mind of someone in the throes of constipation.

Drake Montague, the article began, *is rapidly becoming one of America's hottest young actors after winning the hearts of teenage girls the world over with his performance as Chad, the lovelorn sports-jock in* High School Romeo. *His latest role in* Psychlone, *a sci-fi thriller in which he plays a secret agent with telekinetic powers, is set to make him a major-league star. What's more, our Drake isn't just a devastatingly pretty face – he lists his hobbies as reading, writing, yoga and playing the flute with his dog.*

I turned to Jess in disbelief. '*Playing the flute with his dog?* What is Dad *thinking?*'

I read on.

Unusually for a new arrival on the Hollywood scene, Drake claims to shun the celebrity circuit and says he's keeping an open mind as to the next stage of his career. Nevertheless, our star reporter, BUNNY ANDERSON, got up close and personal with Drake during his recent visit to London for the premiere of Psychlone. *She found the notoriously media-shy star is every bit as charismatic in the flesh as he is on screen – girls, prepare to fall in love all over again!*

BA: Drake, you've only just turned nineteen. How are you coping with the pressure of being fantastic-

*ally good-looking, rich, talented and successful at
such a young age?*

*DM: [laughs modestly] Hey, you're making me
blush! Seriously – I try not to take the hype at face
value. My family and friends keep me grounded.*

*BA: You've come far since your first role as the
little brother in teen drama* Casey's Brook. *What
have you learned along the way?*

*DM: [Pauses for thought] To be true to myself. To
not let other people's negativity get me down . . . I
try to live every day as it comes, I guess.*

*BA: So you're a philosopher as well as a pin-up! Tell
me, Drake, was it the intellectual elements of*
Psychlone *that first attracted you to the script?*

DM: Intellectual elements?

*BA: Well, it's a film about the powers of the mind,
isn't it? Like when you use telepathy to fry the
villain's brain and it melts out of his ears?*

*DM: Actually, it was more of a physical role. I had
to work out a lot. [Flexes his arm]*

BA: And oh boy, does it show . . .

On they droned – Drake confiding how he hoped
one day to meet 'that special someone'; Drake moraliz-
ing on how acting in the prison-camp drama 'reminded
me of how much I have to be thankful for'; Drake
revealing that he was 'looking for new challenges'
and had some 'very exciting' projects lined up . . . He
sounded about as intelligent and charismatic as cold
porridge. I couldn't believe Dad thought this guy was
brimming with talent. Was it possible that my father
had fallen for the charms of Drake's smoky eyes and

chiselled jaw? No – that was ridiculous, I told myself. My father wasn't like that. Of course not. Nonetheless, I began to think of our visit to the film set with increasing dread.

I was hoping for an evening of total collapse, but came home to find my mother trilling away on the telephone about my 'latest conquest'. Apparently, 'just between ourselves', Alex was 'wild' about me and Rich Withers himself was coming to me for advice about his healthy-eating regime.

When she got off the phone I ventured to suggest that my two-minute conversation with R.W. about bacon sandwiches could hardly be described as an intimate dietary consultation, but she dismissed this with a distracted wave of her hand. Then she looked at me reproachfully. 'Now, Octavia, I'm very pleased you went out and had a nice evening with Alexis, but next time you absolutely must let me know what time you're coming back. Or take your mobile with you at least. I mean, *really*!'

'Oh God, I'm sorry—' I began, genuinely stricken. I had completely forgotten.

'Well, never mind that for now. I know you're a sensible girl. But speaking of *sensible*, I was just going through some of your things while you were at school because, really, after that party and with Alexis and everything, I was thinking that it's time for you to, you know, *update* yourself a bit. So I've put in some old things of mine you might want, like that lace top you wore the other night, and a few bits and pieces I picked up in the shops this week (though, honestly, I've bought you so many nice clothes that you hardly *ever* wear). Of course, I do appreciate that style is a very personal matter, but . . .' By now we were both in my room standing in front of the wardrobe. I opened it to find that my clothes seemed to have multiplied and that all of the hangers had little coloured stickers on them.

'Red is for sending to the charity shop, green is for keeping and blue is for reassessment,' my mother explained.

'Reassessment?'

'Yes, I wasn't *quite* sure about these. Maybe if you customize them, get some new accessories or something,' she said vaguely. I noticed that nearly all of the green stickers were on the clothes that my mother had bought me or passed down, whereas most of my usual shirts and jumpers had red stickers on them. There weren't many blue ones.

'I'm not sure I'm the sort of person—' I began.

'Don't be bashful, you funny girl! You've become so *outgoing* these days . . . I'm *proud* of you, darling, and I only want to help. That's what clothes are all about, you know – helping you feel confident for every occasion. Now here's something I bought you ages ago but I've never seen you wearing,' she said, pulling out a dark chocolate-brown angora sweater trimmed with soft little silvery feathers around the neck. 'So charming and a touch *artistic*, wouldn't you say?' It was the kind of thing that India might wear. Hanging next to it was one of my favourite T-shirts. It was a flattering fit and a pretty shade of blue, but I saw what my mother meant. The T-shirt wasn't the type of clothing that would make the sons of rock stars sit up and take notice and escort me around posh nightclubs and coffee bars. I knew I should thank my lucky stars that my mother provided me with the sort of clothing that would – the sort of clothing that was now arrayed, like the plumage of an exotic bird, in my newly organized wardrobe. And yet I felt an odd sense of disloyalty, defeat even, when I took the charity shop bin bag out to the front door.

'Nice sweater.'

'Thanks.'

Alex and I were sitting in the window of a small, brightly painted coffee shop just off the King's Road. The silvery feathers were prickling my neck, and because I was afraid of appearing overdressed I had kept on my scruffiest denim jacket and so was unpleasantly hot. However, by my second cup of coffee I grew reckless and abandoned the jacket, still feeling a bit self-conscious (I imagined Viv's incredulous reaction – 'Is that a feather *boa* you've got round your neck?'). Alex and I were getting along fine, but without a crowd of people around him he seemed ever so slightly uncomfortable.

I wondered if this was because of me, because of something I was doing wrong. Unexpectedly, he answered this himself. 'You know, I'm not used to spending much time on my own. Even with just one other person, even if we're having a good time . . . I suppose I get . . . fidgety without lots of people around.'

'Big groups can be lonely, though. More lonely, sometimes, than being on your own.'

'Maybe, but at least there'll always be a distraction. I'd go crazy with boredom just talking to myself.'

'Don't you find yourself good company then?' I

asked, and then blushed, feeling that the question was silly and maybe rude. He didn't look annoyed, exactly, but he was frowning as if something troubled him. To change the subject I told him that on Thursday I would be flying out to the States for a few days. I was going as my mother's guest to an award ceremony in Los Angeles, but I was careful not to sound like I was trying to make a big deal out of it. Nor was Alex especially interested.

'Really? Good for you. I hope it's not too much of a drag though . . . those sort of events can be quite amusing but they do go *on*.'

Alex appeared to be less impressed by the award ceremony than by the fact that my grandfather is a real live lord. Grandpa Cleeve is apparently on one of the same charity boards as Alex's father. He told me that Rich Withers is tipped for a knighthood in the next honours list. 'My mother will be furious she's missed her chance to bag a title as part of the divorce settlement. Lady Tigerlily Withers and all that. But Dad's been secretly hankering after one for ages – most of his friends have got titles now. The poor old sod's even taken to sponsoring galas at the Royal Opera House.'

I thought of Rich Withers's legendary sex 'n drugs 'n hotel-bedroom trashing days, then tried to imagine he and Lord Clairbrook-Cleeve making small talk between acts at the opera. I failed. I guess my thought showed on my face, because Alex caught my eye and we both started laughing; he had just taken a sip of coffee and nearly choked with trying not to spray it everywhere. It was that silly, spontaneous, private kind of joke that usually only happens between people who know one another very well. Afterwards we wandered around a variety of topics and Alex held forth on his trips to New York and Mustique, where his mother now lives. But every now and then we'd catch each other's eye and start laughing again.

I went for supper at Dad and Michael's, although Dad didn't arrive home until nine and had to leave early the next morning to look over Saturday's rushes with his film editor. While we were waiting for Dad, I made, under Michael's supervision, a chocolate-chestnut cake for pudding. It was a little bit burnt round the edges but Michael showed me how to disguise this by dusting it with icing sugar. 'Nine-tenths of successful cookery is successful presentation,' he said, with a flourish of the sieve.

'You sound like my mother,' I said. 'It's a sad state of affairs when even chocolate cake needs cosmetic improvement.'

He flicked icing sugar at my nose.

'The true beauty of chocolate cake is in the taste buds of the beholder. Shall we try and restrain ourselves and save half for your mum?'

'She's on a diet.'

Over supper, we didn't talk about the Withers family or my visit to the set or even Drake and his 'devastatingly pretty' face, but discussed redecorating the dining room and plans for celebrating Michael's birthday in a couple of weeks' time. It was only when we got to the cake crumbs and coffee stage of the evening that Dad cleared his throat and scratched his head in that parent-about-to-embark-on-a-pep-talk kind of way.

'And how's Alex?'

'He's fine.'

'Has he, er, taken you out anywhere nice lately?'

'We went for coffee this morning. Just chatted and stuff. It was very . . . relaxed.'

'And when will you be seeing him next?'

'Monday, as a matter of fact. I'm meeting him after school at the record company he's working for.'

'Good. That's good.' He cleared his throat again. Michael left the table and made his way to the kitchen with a stack of plates. 'I'm glad that you're enjoying his company. Your mother is certainly very pleased for you. As am I, of course. And so, ah, because we both know how mature you are we don't want to interfere with things . . . don't want to *nanny* you, as it were. But sometimes,' he continued, looking down at his coffee cup, 'it can be reassuring to be nagged. Just a little. Just to know that your aged parents haven't quite given up on being unreasonable, out of touch and paranoid.'

I had to smile at this, though I was shifting uncomfortably on my chair.

'He's a bit older than you, isn't he?' he asked gently.

'Three years. He's eighteen.'

'And you've been out to bars with him? Clubs too?'

'Yes.' I couldn't quite look him in the eye.

'You and I both know that I won't be able to stop you from going to these places and I'm not going to give you a lecture on the evils of underage drinking, either. I expect you're more than capable of working them out for yourself. But I hope very much that Alex . . . that if you said you didn't want to go to a club or have a drink or . . . whatever . . . that Alex would respect your decision. That you would feel comfortable about making that choice. You understand?'

I was crimson with embarrassment, but I nodded.

'OK. Now what are the chances of this paranoid and unreasonable parent being bribed with another slice of cake?'

On Sunday I did some long-overdue homework and then helped Michael to move furniture from the dining room and try out paint samples on the walls. Then I got on the bus and went round to Viv's for tea, where I had a rapturous reception from Mrs Duckworth. She had taped the *Prattler* picture of Alex and me to the fridge – 'Your mother must be so proud! You look *just* like Audrey Hepburn!'

'Yeah, right. If Audrey were six-foot tall with a permanent bad-hair day. And if the person looking at me was standing on the other side of a dark room,' I muttered when we had escaped to Viv's bedroom, 'having lost their glasses. After drinking heavily for several hours.'

'Oi. So what are you saying about my mum?' Viv punched me lightly in the stomach. 'Now tell me about Wednesday. And Saturday too, of course. How's the Prince of Darkness?'

I filled her in. 'And so,' I said in conclusion, 'on the one hand I've got Dad giving me thinly disguised lectures on the Just Say No theme and on the other hand my mother's thrusting me into plunging necklines and telling me not to be such a square. It's only a matter of time before she insists on waxing my eyebrows every Sunday. And gets me chanting "my body is a temple and my face is my fortune" fifty times before breakfast.'

'Well, I hope you set her straight,' Viv said tartly. 'Culturally imposed standards of physical perfection are a major factor in the disempowerment of the female, you know.'

'Yes, but . . . there's nothing wrong with making the most of myself, is there?'

'Hang on – I thought you just complained that your mother was turning into a makeover militant.'

'So maybe I was exaggerating a bit. She is *trying* to help. And Alex seems to appreciate it when I make an effort.'

Viv rolled her eyes. 'I'm sure he does. Plunging necklines do tend to have that effect.' Then she perked up. 'You know what, now that you're such a social butterfly, you've no excuse not to come out with me. There's a joint birthday party with lots of people from school at someone's house on Friday week. I can't promise crown princes or champagne fountains, but I think it's going to be good. And you should come.'

'But I won't know anyone. I'm not invited.'

'Open invitation. And anyway,' she added slyly, 'you could always bring Alex.'

I looked down awkwardly.

'Hmm, thought not. I suppose it's not really his scene – comprehensive-school oiks, cheesy music, cheap beer, warm hearts and all that. Like the minions frolicking about in the third-class decks of the *Titanic*.'

'It's not that – really. It's just I – we – I don't know . . . we're not . . .'

Viv took pity on me. 'It's OK. I guess it's early days.

But I'm still not letting you off the hook, my girl. You are coming.'

It was only when I got home that I realized that the party was on the same Friday as our trip to the film set.

Brimstone Records was located in a shabby backstreet near King's Cross and, like Darlinham House, was apparently too cutting-edge to bother advertising its presence. After checking Alex's directions for the twentieth time and repeatedly trudging back and forth between two equally dingy and anonymous front doors, I finally spied another entrance in the alley to one side of the building. There was a rusty iron grille between the street and the inner door with a Brimstone business card propped inside, but no bell. Perhaps this was a special pop-idol obstacle course, with a million-pound record deal for anyone who actually made it to reception. Or maybe they were secretly recruiting for MI5? I tried Alex's mobile again but to no avail. I was just about to wave my hands in the air and try screaming 'Open Sesame!' when I spotted the buzzer, which had been cunningly fixed at knee level. Finally, after a long crackle of static, somebody mumbled ' 'lo?' through the intercom and I was able to state my name and business. Five minutes after *that* I was buzzed in.

The reception, which you reached at the top of two steep flights of stairs, was a narrow room with an unoccupied desk, a couple of brown-leather beanbags and a sound system throbbing noisily away in the corner. The peeling olive-green walls were nearly buried under a layer of posters and signed photographs of hairy blokes with gloomy expressions. Through the glass partition behind the desk I could see a long cluttered office and a whole gang of Designer Tramps lounging around in a fog of cigarette smoke. There was no sign of Alex. I assumed he must be absorbed in the 'creative process' elsewhere.

Closer inspection of my surroundings revealed that Brimstone Records's peeling paintwork was probably an indication of artistic credibility rather than financial hardship. What I was able to see of the office equipment looked suspiciously shiny and state-of-the-art for a shoe-string operation, and even my mother would have been able to spot several of the gloomy poster-boys for the millionaire chart-toppers they in fact were. There were also a number of gold and platinum edition disks glinting from their presentation frames above the door.

After another ten minutes of hanging around on my own I decided enough was enough. I went through the door in the partition without setting off any alarms and began walking purposefully towards the nearest Designer Tramp, but before I got there Alex himself appeared from another doorway. He looked hot and harassed and was holding a tray full of mugs. 'Right, I've got two black coffees, one white (artificial sweetener), one green tea and one tea with milk and two sugars. Oh, and we're out of decaf.' He put the tray down on the nearest desk with a grunt of relief, then caught sight of me. He didn't look overly thrilled. 'Octavia! God – is that the time already?' Alex took hold of my arm and began to hustle me out of the office. 'Er, bye guys . . .' The Designer Tramps were busy helping themselves to refreshments, but a couple waved their hands at us in a distracted sort of way.

We descended to the street and started walking in silence, Alex leading the way with a faintly embarrassed air. Finally he cleared his throat. 'The really great thing about working in a place like Brimstone is that nobody stands on ceremony, you know?' I nodded encouragingly. 'You might think that being the son of Rich Withers and everything I get used to special treatment . . . but as a matter of fact I find it very, er, liberating to be treated just like everybody else.' I nodded again, but had a feeling that I wasn't the one who needed convincing. 'There's nothing so tedious as people who are overawed by a showbiz connection. You do get used to it, I suppose . . . but of course,' he added, 'someone like you would find that kind of pressure hard to understand.'

'Someone like me? Someone ordinary, you mean?'

'Oh no, not ordinary,' he said hastily, 'you're not *ordinary*. It's just because Dad is . . . whereas your father . . .' I think Alex sensed he was digging himself into a hole, at any rate he stopped outside the entrance to a juice bar with a sigh of relief. 'OK, so here we are. The decor isn't up to much, but it's the best this dump of a neighbourhood can offer.'

To be honest, I would have preferred the greasy spoon two doors down as wheatgrass smoothies aren't really my thing, but I suppose the last thing Alex wanted to see was another mug of tea or coffee. When we were perched on our aluminium stools, a jug of carrot 'n papaya juice between us, I brought the conversation back to something that had been bothering me.

'Alex, would it be so bad if I was . . . normal?'

'What do you mean? There's nothing *ab*normal about you. Not unless there's a scaly tail and an extra toe or two you haven't told me about . . .' He suddenly looked anxious. 'This isn't about a weird eating complex, is it? Because I've never thought you look fat or anything.'

'Sorry, I'm not explaining myself properly. I don't mean normal – I mean average. Ordinary. What if I didn't go to Darlinham House? If my mother was a teacher and my dad worked in a bank, for example? Would we still be sitting here?'

'But if you didn't go to Darlinham House, you wouldn't be friends with Indy and I'd never have met you,' he said impatiently.

'Yes, but say you *had*. Would you still have noticed me? Liked me?'

'Octavia, I didn't mean you or your family were *commonplace*. Look, whatever I said before was just the ramblings of someone who's spent far too long scraping the bottom of a coffee tin. Don't pay any attention to it.' He reached across and took my hand, his dark eyes serious. 'I don't think you're ordinary. I think you're special. Which reminds me . . .' he rummaged in his coat pocket and brought out a small eggshell-blue box. 'Here. It's a little good-luck present for your American trip.'

Inside the box was a tiny mother-of-pearl heart on a gold chain. My own heart was in a happy flutter as he fastened it around my neck and I felt the pendant nestle under my collarbone; even without a mirror I could tell it looked 'just right'. I began to tell Alex all the ways in which I liked it, but in the end put my arms around him and kissed him instead. If this was the first step to becoming a material girl I might as well make the most of being shallow.

'So are you happy now?' he asked, just a touch complacently, after we'd come up for air.

'Well, if you're trying to buy my affections, you're *definitely* on the right track,' I said, toasting him with the carrot and papaya juice.

But after we'd said our goodbyes and I returned home (where my loot sent Lady Jane into raptures of joy), the nagging feeling returned that Alex hadn't really answered, or understood, my question. Alex thought I was 'special', but he also thought I was a bona fide Darling like all the rest. Would I still be special to him if he realized that I was only an impostor, and a half-hearted one at that? And could going out with Alex turn me into the real thing? This having-your-cake-and-eating-it business was becoming more complicated than I'd bargained for.

The next couple of days were taken up with preparations for the trip to LA and the Joy Of Laughter Awards, otherwise known as the 'Jollies'. They're an established event on the American media calendar and began fourteen years ago as a charity event to raise money to send comedians round kids' hospitals with presents and punchlines. The organizers claim to be promoting jollity in 'all the performing arts', but it's mainly film and TV with an award for the best TV sitcom (*Lady Jane's* won this about three times), best sitcom star (step forward, Helena Clairbrook-Cleeve), best comic film, best comic performance in a film, etc., etc. However, comedians/comediennes on the stand-up circuit get a look-in too, as well as stage plays and musicals and there's even one for the funniest advert. Mind you, establishing the criteria for defining 'comic' can be a bit tricky and somebody always kicks up a fuss. The year before last, for instance, a production of *Hamlet* was nominated for something on the grounds that it's actually a black comedy. The British press reported this with much relish, but don't usually bother with the all-American Jollies too much. Since the Jollies want to safe-guard the clean, cosy kind of humour suitable for kids in hospitals, you can mostly predict who's going to win (and no, the *Hamlet* didn't).

My mother, of course, is a Jolly regular, and this year was presenting the award for Outstanding Comic Performance of the Year. And I was going to cheer her on. While I wasn't delirious with excitement at the prospect I thought it could be quite fun – the cere-mony's held at an enormous modern theatre in Beverly Hills, and everyone gets dressed up and sits at little tables for a four-course meal while they're entertained by musicians and top stand-up comics doing their thing. After the meal, you stay at the tables for the award ceremony itself and, since the winners all have a witty reputation to live up to, the acceptance speeches are (mostly) entertaining and tear-free. Then there's a big party afterwards in a swanky hotel.

So, all in all, I was looking forward to it – at least until the question of what to wear was raised. I was kind of hoping I could wear the same thing I wore to India's party or something similar; I'd enjoyed our trip to the vintage dress shop and I wanted to wear those little silk slippers again. But my mother was aghast at my suggestion – 'Darling, you don't wear *jeans* to an award ceremony. I mean, they're not even *designer*! And you've already been photographed in that top!' I started arguing about this, but she held firm. 'Making an effort with your clothes is all about showing *respect,* Octavia. It shows that you're taking this event seriously.'

'And there was me thinking that it was all about comedy,' I muttered. My mother pursed her lips.

'Looking good in this business is no laughing matter.'

Sure enough, our second shopping expedition of the month was not big on laughs. With hindsight, it was obviously a mistake to have left only two days for me to find something to wear; after all, my mother had been planning her outfit for more or less the past six months. However, there was some sort of administrative muddle with her guest tickets and I didn't actually know I was going until a week before the event. (At least the fact that I'd be missing a lot of school at short notice was not a problem. One of the advantages of Darlinham House is that you can do your own thing and mostly get away with it – our teachers don't like to exercise much authority out of deference to the exalted status of their students. Or their students' parents, that is.) We'd originally planned to clothes-hunt at the weekend, but my mother was unexpectedly summoned for a last-minute reshoot for her detective drama and had made it very clear that I couldn't be trusted to go shopping on my own. So there I was on my way to a celebrity j amboree, yet with only two days left to find an outfit that would show the world that I was to the star-spangled manner born. It's a tough life.

The fact that I knew I was being ridiculous and ungrateful about the whole business wasn't helped by my mother continually exhorting me to 'think of the Ordinary People' as I stumped into yet another exquisite clothing emporium. 'Ordinary People' are my mother's equivalent of the starving Africans – all those thousands of poor unfortunates 'who would Give Anything to be in your position'. She conjured up tragic visions of the general public crammed against barriers in sweaty auto-graph-hunting hordes, desperate for a crumb from the celebrity table.

The last time she reminded me of this I was struggling into a dress apparently constructed from a mixture of chiffon and armour plating and with a long ruffled train sequinned in orange and silver. I was bulging out from places I didn't know it was possible to have bulges and my cheeks – purple from the effort of squeezing into the corset top – clashed horribly with the extravagant orange ruffles. Sweat beaded my brow. A sales assistant was cooing sweet nothings in the back-ground. 'To *die* for!' she trilled, insincerity oozing from every pore.

Death, or possibly murder, was certainly on my mind. 'Ordinary people? That's the whole bloody prob-lem,' I snarled somewhat breathlessly. 'I *am* ordinary.'

My mother was shocked. 'Oh, darling! No!' It was like Alex all over again, I thought with a pang. '*Everybody* is special,' she intoned piously.

'So special!' purred the sales assistant.

I think I must have had a dangerous light in my eye,

for my mother hastily shooed away Ms To Die For and started unhooking the corset in a placating manner. 'You can breathe out now, darling. Goodness, this reminds me of my costume-drama days.'

'Don't you mean bodice-ripper days?' I said nastily. My mother had never quite made the Jane Austen grade. She nobly chose to ignore me.

'I think something just a touch less *flamboyant*, perhaps. Now, there was the sweetest little organza slip-dress I saw in that place down the road . . .'

I tried on the slip-dress. I tried on tops, I tried on skirts, I tried on dresses, I tried on trousers. Clothes of every shade and cut, clothes made of organza, chiffon, silk, tulle, velvet, suede, taffeta, satin, lace and combinations of all of these . . . I even tried a sort of poncho thing made out of purple suede and trimmed with the little red plastic nets you get tangerines in – 'Deliciously ironic!' said the sales assistant. It was after I'd experimented with this, on the final day of our clothes quest, as evening was drawing on and shop managers were getting that actually-we're-just-about-to-close air, that I began to think that I wouldn't be going to the award ceremony after all. Even Lady Jane was looking a little shop-worn.

'Just *one* last place, darling! It's only round the corner.' She turned into a cul-de-sac that looked as if it should be in the heart of a country village instead of five minutes' walk from the Brompton Road. The little Victorian houses were painted in pretty pastel shades, the road was cobbled and there was an old-fashioned street lamp made of wrought iron. However, there was nothing in the least old-fashioned about the boutique, which was one of those places where you have to ring the bell and they inspect you through the glass before they decide whether or not you're up to the standards of their establishment. I kept well in the background.

'Actually, madam, we were just about to close—'

Lady Jane smiled her most aristocratic smile: peaches 'n cream with a hint of iceberg. It seldom fails. 'Don't worry at all. You just carry on with whatever you need to do – we won't be *any* trouble.' She sailed on, me trailing behind her, into a room like all the others, with chilly white walls and a chilly polished floor and a chilly polished manageress. The only warmth or colour in the place was in the racks of clothes, a glittering, rainbow-rich profusion of fabrics and dyes. Bitter experience had taught me that this abundance was deceptive; that flashy, flimsy frocks need flashy, flimsy people to wear them, not hulking great obelisks. But my mother was relentless. 'Now then, what about this?'

I sighed and began to trot out the inevitable 'It's-lovely-but-no-thanks-it's-not-my-colour/cut/fit/style'. Then I actually looked at it. She was holding up a simple silk trouser suit of the most beautiful colour I had ever seen: an opulent, intense azure shot through with still deeper shades of blue and the turquoise shimmer of a peacock's tail.

'Well? What do you think? Worth a try?'

I crossed my fingers tightly. Please, please, let this be the one. Let this fit. I had a glorious vision of finally escaping the boutique in a flurry of tissue paper and glossy bags, of supper in front of the television followed by a hot bath . . . of that gleaming silk safely stowed away in my wardrobe . . . of Alex, perhaps, catching sight of me in some TV or newspaper report, floating down a red carpet, resplendent in my peacock finery . . .

I went to the fitting room in a daze. The assistant had gone and only the manageress was left, drumming her fingers on the desk and looking chillier by the minute. I put on the jacket very slowly, very carefully and then very slowly pulled on the trousers. They were, incredibly, the perfect length and the jacket clung in all the right places. The lustrous blue deepened and shimmered with every movement. I went out to show my mother.

'Hmmn, yes. Yes,' she said, walking around me with a slight frown of concentration on her face. 'Of course, it would look even better with a tan . . . but that colour's really rather nice. And the trousers could have been tailor-made for you. Yes. How do you feel about it?'

I looked in one of the mirrors. I didn't really want to look at my face, I was feeling grey and smudged and dishevelled. I just concentrated on the blue. And the slight, silken, reassuring weight of the jacket on my shoulders.

'I like it,' I finally said.

My mother's sigh of relief sent the gauzy scarves a-fluttering on the rail.

'*Wonderful.*' Then she shoved me back into the fitting room and practically undressed me herself in her hurry to get the suit to the till and paid for before I could change my mind. When the manageress saw that we were actually buying something she thawed enough to ask if there was anything else she could help us with.

'Yes, there is in fact,' said my mother. The manageress's smile returned to its permafrost setting. 'Shoes. We need shoes for the suit. Something like those.' She gestured to some strappy sandal-type things with heels. I started to protest. Then I saw the glint of steel in her eyes. 'Don't even *think* about it, Octavia. What else are you going to wear with an outfit like this? Flip-flops? Loafers?'

'But—'

'*Octavia*. Darling. It has been a long day. For both of us. I want you to take a deep breath and trust me on this one.' She closed her eyes for a moment and put her hand to her brow. 'We are going to an award ceremony. People will be dressed up. The women will all wear heels. There will be a party afterwards, most likely attended by models as well as actors. Most of the models will be six-foot tall. Most of them will be wearing six-inch heels. My own shoes are stilettos. So for once, just once, I'm going to ask you to forget about your height fixation and allow me to buy you some new shoes. OK?'

We bought the shoes.

That was on Wednesday. On Thursday we flew out to the States and were picked up from the airport by a limousine provided by the Jolly organizers. My mother has a little flat in downtown LA that she uses when she's filming, but since she was presenting an award, all our expenses were paid for by the Joy Of Laughter Guild or whatever it was and this included being put up in a swish hotel not far from where the ceremony was taking place. My favourite style of hotel is the romantically antique kind with lots of red-velvet drapery, marble and chandeliers (what Dad calls the 'luxury brothel' style), but this one was ultra-modern: all gleaming white walls and slippery glass surfaces and polished steel. We had a suite with two double rooms, a bathroom and a living room, all done in varying shades of white (so if you think that white only comes in one colour, you'd be wrong). Doubtless India would approve of the colour scheme, but I felt that I left smudges everywhere.

The best part of grand hotels is the bathrooms. This one was nearly as big as our living room at home and had a whirlpool jacuzzi and the kind of power shower that's strong enough to leave little dents all over your skin. The towels were so thick and soft it was like wrapping yourself in a cloud. You could choose between a slinky silk dressing gown and a big velvety one that made you look like a polar bear. Someone had also thoughtfully provided each of us with a basket of posh bath lotions and creams and powders, which I emptied into my suitcase to take back for Viv.

After I'd padded out from the bathroom in a cloud of perfumed steam, trailing the hem of my polar-bear robe in the various puddles I'd created, I went to the living room to find my mother cooing over a huge bouquet of golden roses that had just been delivered. Not very original, but at least they were a cheerful colour. The hotel had furnished us with a vase full of white orchids that were so perfect, so exquisitely frozen-looking it was hard to believe that they were real. The Jolly Guild had sent a gaudy basket of exotic fruit. Then several of my mother's American friends or people who worked with her on her show had also sent flowers and cards and boxes of luxury chocolates.

Once my mother had floated off to the bathroom I sneaked a look at the note that came with the roses: *Welcome back to the US, Princess! Looking forward to Saturday night, x Bud*. In spite of sharing a name with a beer, or maybe a Labrador puppy, Bud was some kind of executive in the Tempest Television Company and my mother's other guest for the ceremony on Saturday night. I remembered that Viv's mum had cut out a newspaper clipping for me not so long ago that described my mother as being 'squired' by Budwin Carnaby to some American media event, as if she were a medieval damsel or something. Would a newspaper columnist ever describe Alex as 'squiring' me? Would Alex welcome me back to the UK with bouquets of flowers or baskets of tropical fruit? I fingered my pearly heart and smiled. Then I caught my reflection in the mirror and realized that if I looked any soppier I'd be a puddle of syrup.

I would have preferred to stay collapsed on the sofa for the rest of the evening, picking my way through the chocolates and the television channels. My mother, unfortunately, had other ideas and was expecting some of her 'dearest, dearest' LA cronies to pop round for an informal soirée. Ever since we'd got to the airport she'd been knocking back this vile khaki-coloured vitamin drink that claims to make you immune to jetlag and now she was raring to move on to the bubbly. Barely an hour after we'd been shown to our suite I was packed off to brush up my party manners and change into a charcoal silk skirt and the lace top I'd worn to the Rah Bar. I even tried some of the vitamin drink in an attempt to reach the levels of perkiness required, but it only made me gag.

Our guests arrived laden with yet more flowers and chocolates and mega-watt smiles. There were a couple who I didn't recognize, but most of them were familiar to me from similar occasions: Quentin Braithwaite, one of my mother's co-stars on *Lady Jane*; her agent, Frisbee; an expat (and genuine aristocrat) called Harmonia, and the chat-show host Suzi Sanmartini. Plus Suzi's latest squeeze – not for nothing is she known as 'Floozie' in the media world. I tried to appear wholly occupied with my responsibilities as self-appointed waitress, but my plan was foiled by the real waiter, who didn't take kindly to me sneaking off with his tray of canapés. After a brief tussle with him behind the piano I acknowledged defeat and slunk back to join the party.

'*There* you are, darling!' said my mother gaily. 'Come and say hello to everyone. You remember Octavia, don't you, Suzi?'

'Now will you look at that!' cooed Suzi. 'She's turned into quite a doll! When did you go and get so grown up, hon?' Her mouth was as lacquered-looking as her hair and she was wearing a salmon-pink suit so tight that every movement she made had a wiggle in it. Her question didn't seem to require an answer, however, as she immediately turned her back on me and continued her conversation with the man-of-the-moment. I think his name may have been Ralph, but as he didn't utter a word to anyone except for Suzi the whole evening it was hard to be sure. He looked at least ten years younger than her and had a rather dazed expression.

My moment in the spotlight was not over yet, alas. Harmonia wafted over and we exchanged kisses. I never understand the rules on this – do you go left to right cheek or right to left? One kiss or two? – but in spite of looking as exquisitely fragile as one of the orchids, Harmonia is a lady who likes to take charge. It was more of a brisk 'peck-peck' than an air-kissy 'mwah-mwah'. Then she turned to my mother.

'Congratulations, Helena. She looks like she'll be a true Clairbrook-Cleeve.' I'm not sure either my mother or I quite knew what to make of this, but Lady Jane obviously decided to take it as a compliment.

'That's so sweet of you,' she said. 'Her, er, grand-father is certainly very proud.'

'Yes, humility has never been his strong point. Life's not been the same since the good old days when peasants really knew how to grovel,' I added before I could stop myself. My mother shot me an evil look, but Quentin joined in before she could take it further.

'Ah, humility! *Not* a quality with which this town is familiar,' he sniffed. 'Some might say, indeed, that there's a *national* shortage.' Quentin came to Hollywood nearly thirty years ago with great hopes of fame as the Dashing English Gentleman. He soon discovered that his cut-glass accent had combined with the arch in his eyebrow and the curl in his lip to doom him to a small-screen career of playing butlers and villains. He is a very bitter man but quite a good comic actor and his snobbish-yet-soft-hearted butler is one of the best things about *Lady Jane*. My mother tells me that hundreds of American housewives send him their knickers through the post.

'Speaking of quality,' said someone, though we hadn't been really, 'have you *seen* Bambi Luxmoore's new game show? The one where she picks out random people from the street and they compete for plastic-surgery prizes? I saw the "before" and "after" interviews with the fat Mexican girl who won the nose job and it was so touching I *cried*.'

'Oh, I know,' chimed in somebody else, 'Bambi's such a honey. I met her daughter the other day and she was just *delightful* as well. She's all set to follow in her mom's footsteps, you know, though she's only seventeen.'

'She's got her own newspaper column and everything, about her social life as a "Tinsel Town Teen". They say she's going out with a Kennedy,' put in Frisbee. A Kennedy male is apparently the American equivalent of Prince Richard, for a reverent hush descended on the room. Even the waiter looked impressed.

'Actually,' said my mother, drawing herself up a bit, 'as a matter of fact, *Octavia* is going out with Rich Withers's son. Rich Withers from *Spilt Milk,* you know.' She beamed round at everybody in a triumphant sort of way. They all turned and stared and I felt myself flush.

'My-oh-my,' said Suzi at last, looking me over again, but more carefully this time. 'I hope the son's not as much of a rascal as his daddy. You be sure to keep him on a tight leash, hon.' She gave me a chummy smile. 'Or maybe you like the wild boys?'

There was an expectant pause. 'But Alex isn't . . . I'm not . . . well, sometimes I do feel a bit out of my depth,' I mumbled.

'Don't be *ridiculous*, sweetheart,' said my mother, her smile a little fixed. 'You know Alex is crazy about you. He gave you that gorgeous necklace you're wearing, didn't he? As a "bon voyage" gift, just before we left,' she explained to the rest.

'Lucky girl!' said Frisbee admiringly.

'What a catch,' murmured somebody else. Quentin merely sniffed.

'I remember,' mused Harmonia, 'how I once sneaked off from school to sleep on the pavement outside a hotel where *Spilt Milk* were staying . . . it must have been during their "Arsenic Angel" tour. Then as they were leaving I ran up and got Rich to sign my breasts in red lipstick. It got into the papers, and poor Mummy was *furious*.'

After this revelation the conversation moved on to tales of deranged groupies and the weird fan mail people got sent, much to my relief (if not, perhaps, Quentin's). But as people were leaving, I heard Frisbee say to my mother, 'So Octavia's with Alexis Withers? Well done her! Of course, she's grown up so much since I last saw her – she looks quite charming.'

'Oh, but I always knew she would be,' said my mother fondly, 'once she got through that *awkward* phase. And as soon as she gets a bit more confidence . . .'

Then what? I get my own 'Tinsel Town' column and my life will be complete? It was slightly insulting the way everybody always assumed that *I* was the lucky one and that Alex was the prize, the wonderful catch. Nobody, including my mother, seemed to think that Alex was due any congratulation for being with *me*. I found myself wishing, sugar roses and mother-of-pearl hearts notwithstanding, that Alexis Withers could be plain old, boring old Alex Smith.

*

On Friday my mother was away all day at a *Lady Jane* meeting and then a rehearsal for the ceremony, so I was left to my own devices. She suggested, without a hint of irony, that I arrange for a hotel driver to take me shopping.

I was still groggy from jetlag and didn't feel like doing the LA tourist trail on my own, so I restricted my explorations to the hotel itself. I poked my nose in the gym and sauna and had a dip in the indoor swimming pool, then wandered through miles of silent corridors, feet sinking soundlessly into the snowy carpet, and seeing hardly anyone except for chambermaids and porters. I had lunch from room service, which I would have enjoyed more if I hadn't eaten quite so much chocolate and strange spiky fruit from the basket before it arrived. I thought about trying on the trouser suit again, but felt an odd, nervous superstition about wearing it before the event. Then I rode up and down in the lift in the hotel's main atrium a few times, which sucked you up past what felt like hundreds of storeys with dizzying speed, and had glass walls so you could look down and around the expanse of curving glass and steel and gleaming white surfaces. I felt as if I were in an escape pod or space shuttle on the set for a sci-fi film. Like Drake Montague in *Psychlone*, perhaps, getting ready to fry somebody's brains with the devastatingly pretty power of his thoughts . . . After that I dawdled in the lobby, pretending to browse in the hotel's boutiques. I may have been paranoid, but I thought that the shop assistants and security people were looking at me oddly. Maybe I shouldn't have gone up and down in the lift quite so many times.

I telephoned Viv when I got back to our suite. It was about ten-thirty p.m. at home, but it was a Friday night, after all.

'How's the land of the free?' she asked.

'Luxurious, but the awards people are paying. The hotel staff think I'm a loony though. A loony with a lift fixation.'

'I thought they called them elevators over there.'

'Whatever.'

'So it's grim up North America?'

This is what I love about Viv. She never, ever tells me how lucky I am or gives me the General Public's version of Lady Jane's think-of-the-ordinary-people spiel.

'Oh, it's fine. I'm fine. Really. It's just . . . I wish Alex had called.'

'Then it's about time you joined the twenty-first century. Come on, Octavia, you're not a shrinking Victorian violet, so why the hell are you waiting for a man to call the shots? Maybe *he's* waiting to hear from *you*.'

This is what I *don't* love about Viv. She's very good, remorseless even, about making me face uncomfortable facts. Like the fact that I'm a shrinking, snivelling Victorian violet at heart. I sighed.

'You're right. I'll call him.'

'Not in that voice, I hope. He'll think you're phoning to break the news of a death in the family.'

After I said goodbye to Viv ('see yah later, elevator') I tried Alex's mobile number. I got the answerphone. Several times. So I went back to the swimming pool and lingered there until I went soft and limp as a peeled prawn. I think I spent a bit *too* long there, actually, as I felt a bit woozy when I finally emerged, blinking, and with shrivelled fingertips. Finally, I took an hour to drink a toffee-pecan-mocha-frothichino in one of the hotel's cafe-bars while I wondered why I hadn't got through to Alex. No reception? Already gone to bed? Or out and about and too busy to answer?

I had a sudden vision of Alex moping over a vodka tonic in the Rah Bar, and of WeeWee leaning towards him tenderly. 'Never mind, Lex darling, *I'll* not desert you . . .' Then he'd look up at her in a vulnerable, lost sort of way and—

No. I was *not* going to think like this. I was absolutely completely utterly one-hundred-per cent confident that Alex was safely tucked up in bed by now. Alone. And dreaming of my return.

We started our cosmetic preparations for the Jollies just after Saturday's extra-low-fat, high-energy lunch. My mother had a stylist come over to do her hair and make-up and lace her into her dress, but before she embarked on that we each had a facial and a manicure and pedicure. I was glad about the facial because today of all days I'd woken up with a spot. On the side of my jaw. Better than on my nose or the middle of my chin, but not somewhere where my hair could hide it.

I couldn't help feeling that the spot was an omen. There it was, stubborn and red, and no amount of expensive potions and lotions were going to fix it. My mother, of course, looked blooming – skin flawless, eyes radiant – even before she'd been lathered in creams and powdered and scented and delicately tinted from a huge array of pots and paints. It took a long time for her to be fitted into her dress, as the stylist and her assistant fluttered around tweaking and fussing and taking tiny tucks in the material so that its folds fell just right.

I got changed away from them all, in the bathroom, in private. All morning I'd had a feeling of vague unease about the suit that I'd tried to pretend wasn't there, or was just general dissatisfaction because of the spot. It was nagging me that I'd only tried the suit on once, briefly, at the last minute of a long day. I kept going to the wardrobe to remind myself of that gorgeous blue, but something didn't feel quite . . . right. I finally buttoned up the jacket in a rush of defiance and nervousness.

It was still beautiful. It was a truly beautiful suit. Once I'd got it on, the azure silk was just as glowingly rich, just as peacock-shimmering as I remembered. The cut of the jacket and trousers was just as perfect a fit, just as sharp as it had looked in the boutique. The problem was me. I'd hardly looked at my face that evening in the shop when I was so tired and dishevelled and now, when I was well rested, my hair trimmed and tweaked, my make-up perfectly applied, I saw what was wrong. My small features looked uncertain, lost – overwhelmed by that lustrous blue. I looked too . . . young. Like I was play-acting in dressing-up clothes designed for an adult. Not necessarily for someone a lot older than me, but designed for someone assured and maybe a little tough-looking, with cool, confident eyes and razor-sharp cheekbones to match the razor-sharp lines of the suit. Not for me with my pale, young, anxious face, not for someone hunched to disguise their height, and standing awkwardly in shoes they didn't know how to walk in.

I hobbled into the living room, feeling more and

more like lamb dressed as designer mutton. The stylist and her assistant had gone and my mother was standing there putting the last touches to her lipstick. She was wearing a pale sea-green and silver frock with a low back and folds of foamy gauze. She reminded me of a picture in a book about a mermaid which she used to read to me when I was little.

'You look beautiful.'

'Doesn't she just? A real princess.' The speaker was a big blond man who'd risen from his chair and was coming across the room to shake hands with me. 'I'm Bud. Glad to know you, Octavia.' He had a tanned, good-humoured face and was good-looking in that absolutely symmetrical, square-jawed, cleft-chinned, comic-book-hero kind of way. 'Damn, but I'm a lucky guy to be the escort of two such genuine English beauties.' He shook his head admiringly. I was tempted to ask him if he'd had a bad experience with English impostors or maybe just insincere beauties, but Princess Helena was rustling over to inspect the goods.

'Lovely, darling. Such a flattering fit. And really,' she said sotto voce, drawing me to one side, 'you *barely* notice the spot!'

The evening improved once we were in the theatre and I was able to sit back and enjoy events without having to think about what I was doing or looking like. For me, the worst bit was when we got out of the limo and had to walk along the red carpet past the jostle of journalists and excitable fans. During our ill-fated shopping expedition I'd reminded my mother, through gritted teeth, that It Wasn't The Oscars, but even if it was more like Oscar's fifth cousin three-times removed, there was still a fair amount of fanfare and flashing cameras. I would probably have appreciated this more if I wasn't feeling so horribly awkward in the suit and shoes, so I skulked along with my head down, taking care to be behind Bud as much as possible. Luckily, the red-carpet-and-canopy thing was erected along the side of the building, so the press pack was only to one side of us; in spite of my heels, Bud was big enough to provide me with a sort of cover. Once we'd got safely into the foyer of the theatre, though, and my mother had given one last wave to the cameras, she turned and hissed in my ear, 'For goodness sake, stop *bobbing around*, Octavia! You're making me nervous!'

The awards ceremony itself was quite fun though it seemed to go on for hours and hours. It was held in a big state-of-the-art theatre with a special new kind of auditorium that could be arranged so that there was room for lots of little tables to be put in front of the stage. My mother and I, Bud, and the producer of *Lady Jane* and his wife all sat at one table where we were served with several courses of very decorative and rather fiddly food while we listened to stand-up comics and a band. Then there was the token serious speech in which a plea for donations to the Joy Of Laughter Cause was got over with as soon as was decently possible. After the tables were cleared and the images of sick children smiling at clowns disappeared from the screens, the real business of the evening began. Lots of speeches, lots of fancy lighting effects, lots of fanfare, lots of applause, lots of clips from lots of shows . . . most of which I'd never heard of.

My mother was on last because she was presenting the Best In Show award. I was surprised to feel a faint tremor of nerves on her behalf, but of course she was a pro, opening the fateful envelope with breathless excitement and revealing the name inside with all the solemnity of someone announcing a breakthrough cure for AIDS. When the lucky winner went on stage to collect his statuette of the Laughing Fat Man, she cooed and hugged him and clasped her hands in delight as if nothing on this earth could make her more joyful and proud.

We all clapped and cheered like mad too, of course. Bud turned to me, still clapping away with palm-tingling vigour. 'Your mom,' he announced solemnly, 'is a truly gracious and wonderful lady.'

I'll swear the man had tears in his eyes.

The after-ceremony party was held in the type of hotel I'd been hoping for. Red velvet, marble, chandeliers and champagne galore. There were a few genuinely famous faces, but mostly it was the kind of media 'personalities' who you know you recognize from somewhere but you're not sure where or why. My mother was soon surrounded by a braying horde of people, some of whom had been at our little soirée and I should probably have said hello to, but my horrible heels were giving me backache and I decided to go and lurk in the ladies' cloakroom for a bit. I felt a bit sorry for my ole buddy Bud, who was looking after my mother with lost puppy-dog eyes, but I didn't much feel like hanging around to sing the chorus of the Helena Clairbrook-Cleeve Admiration Anthem with him.

It was only when I was washing my hands at the marble basin in the ladies' loo that I realized I had managed to goop something on to the front of my jacket. Even if I was never going to wear the wretched thing again it seemed a pity to spend the rest of the night with what looked like a toxic bird dropping on my lapel. For some insane reason I rubbed at it with a bit of loo roll rather than the scented linen napkins provided. The result was I now had grubby frayed specks of toilet paper down the front of my suit. Very sophisticated, Octavia. Thank God Alex wasn't here to see it.

'Jim? Or is it George?'

It took a moment to realize someone was speaking to me.

'I know! It's Dave, isn't it?' WeeWee's face had magically appeared beside my own in the mirror. It was as if just thinking about Alex had conjured her up, like some evil fairy. She smiled.

I couldn't speak for a moment, just stared in dismay. Even before I'd looked in the mirror I'd known that by this stage of the evening my hair would be going in every direction but the right one and my make-up would have started to get that slightly smudgy, end-of-the-party look. I was glaringly conscious of the spot on my chin and the even bigger one on my lapel. WeeWee, by contrast, looked as polished as if she'd just stepped off the page of a fashion magazine. She was wearing a gold strapless dress that showed off her sun-kissed skin to the best possible advantage, her chestnut hair was coiled in a complicated knot from which only carefully designated tendrils escaped, and her lips shimmered with gold-dusted lipstick.

'Wh-what are you doing here?' I finally managed to ask, none too graciously. In the normal course of things I would be delighted that she was a whole continent away from Alex, but I'd always assumed that this would involve her being a whole continent away from me too.

'I'm a Face of Joy.' She didn't look particularly blissful to me. Smug, certainly. I put my hand up to the mother-of-pearl heart, as if for reassurance, but remembered I'd left it at the hotel after deciding it didn't go with the suit. Oh well – perhaps the next time I ran into WeeWee I'd try brandishing a crucifix.

'The sponsors, you know.'

I still didn't get it. 'Sponsors?'

'Yars. Joy. It's a new pahfume we're launching tonight . . . Naice outfit, by the way. It's mah'vlous how well you suit the androgynous look – so few gals can carry it orff.' She checked her pout in the mirror, then turned to go. 'It's been *rally* fun seeing you heah, Jo. Lex will be *so* amused when I tell him.'

I slunk out of the loos a few minutes after her. Sure enough, there in the main reception room was a large, gold-coloured banner with 'Joy!' written on it in a curly script. I hadn't realized that it was advertising anything other than the awards themselves, but now I took a closer look at the image below. It was a photograph of two girls and a guy jumping up for the sheer joy of being shiny happy people paid squillions just to look good. One of the jolly jumpers had flowing chestnut hair and gold-dusted lips parted in an ecstatic grin. A thought occurred to me and I looked in my handbag for the velvet pouch that had been set by my plate as a goody bag for guests at the ceremony. Inside was a silver charm in the shape of a comic mask and, sure enough, a little perfume bottle. Eau de WeeWee.

The row began when my mother came into the hotel bathroom and found me pouring my little dose of joy down the toilet, a mirthless smile on my lips.

'I just don't understand you, Octavia.'

'So I've noticed.' I was scrubbing my hands to get rid of any lingering scent from my skin.

'No, really I don't. I think that perfume was a *lovely* thought on the part of the organizers. A lovely little memento of the evening. And you're just throwing it back in their face!' She was quite upset.

'I'm not. I'm throwing it down the toilet. I wouldn't dream of throwing it in anybody's face. It might blind them.' I wiped my hands and chucked the bottle into the bin. 'And it isn't a lovely little thought. It's a cynical marketing ploy riding on the back of a charitable cause.'

My mother drew herself up and looked at me sternly. Then, suddenly, her face softened and took on an infinitely wise and forbearing expression.

'Never mind, darling. This is all about Bud, isn't it?' She spoke in a gentle, sickroom kind of voice.

'Bud?' I stared at her. 'What's he got to do with any-thing?'

'It's all right, Octavia. I know these things are com-plicated. But the one thing I want you to know is that my love for you—'

'Stop. Wait.' A picture of Bud's noble brow and manly grin beaming over our breakfast table had appeared in my head with horrible clarity. 'Bud's not the issue here. Really. Though it might be tricky accommodating his surname, of course . . . how would you do it? Helena Carnaby-Clairbrook-Cleeve? Or Helena Clairbrook-Cleeve-Carnaby?

'Octavia—'

'Or maybe Helena Clairbrook-Carnaby-Cleeve,' I mused. 'Might be a tight squeeze on the credits, but you could always—'

'*Octavia*. I don't know what's got into you tonight, but I don't like it.' She took a deep breath. 'Now, we've got a long flight tomorrow. I think we're both tired and should go to bed before we spoil what has been a very wonderful, very special evening. An evening we should be very *thankful* for. Think of the or—'

'I AM THINKING OF THE ORDINARY PEOPLE.' We stood there glaring at each other. Then, very quietly, 'I just don't see what's so bad about being normal. Some people might even . . . like it,' I muttered.

'Of course there's nothing wrong with being ordinary. It's certainly not difficult.' My mother's tone was brusque. Then she sighed, and spoke more gently. 'I gather that for whatever reason you haven't found the last couple of days easy. OK, so now you know that it takes time and effort to be something more than ordinary, and sometimes you can put in all of this and it *still* doesn't go according to plan. And you've got more to lose because you've got more at stake. And you don't like it. But think about this, Octavia. You like Alex and he likes you, right?'

'Yes, but he—' *He doesn't know what I'm really like,* I said to myself as my mother swept on, *and when I'm with him I'm not too sure either.*

'You want things to work out with him, don't you? Yes? Well, in that case you're going to have to get used to going to places and being around people who aren't "ordinary". Maybe he'll take you to some big event like tonight. You'll want to feel comfortable with him. You'll want to feel like you fit in.' She smiled at me a little sadly. 'I really do understand that this doesn't come without effort. It takes time, energy and *practice*, you see. But all relationships do, in their different ways, and it will get easier as you go along. I promise.'

She was right. I hated to admit it, but she was right. If I chose to try and make a go of things with Alex I was choosing bright lights and bouquets and champagne cocktails. I was also choosing scary boutiques and red carpets and shoes with evil, back-torturing heels. And the company of people like India and Suzi and WeeWee. Oh joy.

We got home at half-past three on Monday morning. I was back in school just after lunch, still feeling extremely jetlagged, but I thought I'd better make a long-overdue appearance in the class register. When I came home I had a short nap, drank about half a pint of espresso and then got ready to go out with Alex. All I really wanted to do was go to bed, but I'd made a resolution to grit my teeth, strap on my heels and practise my party smile. This resolution was encouraged by the 'welcome home' bouquet of exotic hothouse blooms delivered to me that morning and which I thought more than made up for the lack of telephone contact over the last week. Lady Jane didn't comment on the flowers, just gave them a Meaningful Look.

Alex was taking me to the launch party of a new bar/restaurant in Hoxton that was also going to function as a gallery for contemporary conceptual art. Apparently his mother was a sponsor or shareholder or something. He told me over the telephone that Tigerlily was 'passionately committed to the British art scene' but unfortunately had to miss the opening because she was in Monaco this week – 'Boo Swartzburger's white tie and tiara ball, you know.' I didn't, but said 'oh, but of course' in an understanding sort of way. I was quite relieved not to be meeting the ex-Mrs Withers, who was doubtless an older version of India, only scarier.

After much soul (and wardrobe) searching, I decided that the trousers from the ill-fated Jolly suit might deserve a second chance if I could find the right sort of top. I finally settled on a plain black halter neck. The spot, I was glad to see, was nearly gone. I tried on all my shoes twice before admitting defeat: my mother was right, I had to wear heels. At least I could sort of walk in them now and as long as I didn't stray far from Alex I wouldn't look too ridiculous. Or so I hoped. Then, just as Alex phoned to say he was waiting outside, I had a last-minute crisis of nerves – if it was a trendy art gallery maybe nobody was going to dress up. They would probably all be slurping caviar in frayed jeans and grubby trainers and shirts from charity-shop bins.

Well, they might have been, but as it happened we never made it to the launch party. We got lost. Alex wasn't in a taxi this time and had roared up to our door in the sleek, black convertible I'd always imagined him in, but although his car was an up-to-the-minute model of an up-to-the-minute range, it did not appear to be equipped with an A-to-Z of London. It also appeared that Alex had forgotten the address and directions for the launch party and had put the wrong contact telephone number in his mobile. So we drove around the fringes of Shoreditch for about an hour and a half, stopping every so often to ask a passer-by if they knew where 'The Hole' was. I think the name of the place was unfortunate. I don't think the big shiny car helped much either. At any rate, we got a lot of abuse along the lines of 'I can tell you in which hole you can shove your *! #*! *# questions/car/face . . .'

Even after the tea-making incident at Brimstone Records I'd found it difficult to imagine Alex as anything other than cool, calm and collected, but there was sweat on his brow and a slightly frantic look in his eye by the time we finally admitted defeat. Somehow we eventually got back on a road we recognized and where Alex was able to illegally park the car not far from a fast-food outlet.

Both of us were absolutely starving by this point as well as tired (me) and irritable (Alex). Alex nobly refrained from taking out his frustration on me, though the girl at our till wasn't so lucky. 'Do you think she has learning disabilities or does she just not understand English?' he asked me in a loud whisper after he'd had to repeat our order. It was quite busy but we managed to find a booth in a quiet corner upstairs where we could settle down to our Super-Deluxe-Mega-Bonanza-Burgers with fries. Alex brooded over his milkshake for a bit, then ran his hands through his hair and gave a slightly embarrassed laugh.

'What?'

'Oh, I don't know. Us. Here. All dolled up and nowhere to go.' We did look a little out of place in that plastic yellow booth, me in my silk trousers, Alex sleek in expensive black. '*Christ*, what a mess I've made of tonight. What an idiot. I'm really sorry, Octavia.'

'It's not a mess. I like it here.' My Bonanza-Burger was surprisingly good; I'd kicked off my shoes and was starting to feel warm and sleepy. I was at ease with myself and my surroundings in a way I hadn't felt for some time. Would Alex understand if I told him that I never really wanted to go to the launch party anyway? I licked mustard off my fingers. 'Welcome to how the other half lives. Look upon it as a crash-course in social realism.'

Alex was fiddling with his straw and frowning. 'Is that what you think I am? Just another spoilt rich kid, I mean? Because sometimes I think that's all I am, too.'

I realized with a start that he was looking to me for reassurance. *Alex*, the dauntingly self-possessed, the effortlessly confident! I felt a rush of relief and also tenderness towards him. I felt quite maternal. 'I wouldn't be here if that's all I thought you were.'

'Truly? It's just that the people I know . . . girls I've taken out . . . even my parents . . . well, sometimes I get this feeling that everything that's important to them is so . . . trivial. And I guess a lot of people would look at me and dismiss me as superficial as well. I used not to mind – I mean, superficial can be fun, right? I always thought that deep down, where it *counted*, I wasn't really like that anyway. Whereas now . . . Maybe I am just like the rest of them. But you're different.'

Ha! I knew it! Alex wasn't just a smouldering sex

god with a nice line in black T-shirts – he had Self-Knowledge and Depth. *And* he liked me because I was different! *And* he didn't want to be superficial! He wanted to *change*! This was a turning point: the crux of our whole relationship. It wouldn't be long now, I told myself triumphantly, until we'd be rid of India and Jools and WeeWee and Suzi and the rest of the glamour junkies. At last we'd be free to do our own thing in peace, to be just another teenage couple drinking milkshakes in a burger bar. I beamed at him across the table.

'So shall I get you an application form for the Bonanza-Burger recruitment fair? It's never too late to enter the University of Real Life, you know. And after we cut up your credit cards we'll go trade in that nice shiny car of yours for a nice shiny tube pass.'

'If that's the sort of re-education you have in mind, I think I'll stick to my fairy-tale life as an international playboy, thank you very much.' He cocked an eyebrow at me and grinned. 'Back to trivia, then – tell me about your trip to LA. How was the award ceremony? I didn't spot you in any of the papers.'

'Try page four of *Stellar!* in their "What Not to Wear" column . . . That was a joke, by the way.'

'Oh. Right.' He didn't seem to have found it wildly funny, but at least he didn't mention being '*so* amused' by WeeWee's report of our encounter either. Then he informed me ('while we're on the subject of international playboys') that he'd had a call that morning from an old friend in Rome and had decided to fly out tomorrow for a couple of days. I couldn't help wondering if this old friend was female, but tried to look pleased for him. 'And I've been thinking about what we were saying last week about crowds and being alone. I think you were right.'

'About what?'

'Well, you didn't say it exactly but I think I know what you meant. That maybe it's better to know a few people and *really* know them. That maybe it's possible to know too many people. You can get too . . . lazy about knowing each other, liking each other even.'

This seemed fairly obvious to me, but Alex announced it as if he'd reached a major breakthrough in social science. He looked at me a bit shyly. I felt like I did about his enthusiasm at the gig – surprised and oddly touched. 'So you're searching for a few select buddies to swap skeletons in closets with, warts and all?'

'Skeletons can be picturesque. I try to avoid warts where at all possible.'

I fell asleep in the car on the way back home as the jetlag finally caught up with me. I woke up to find Alex bending over me somewhat anxiously. 'We're outside your flat but I didn't want to wake you. You looked so peaceful.' I smiled at him sleepily and closed my eyes again. It was a very comfortable car. 'Come on, Sleeping Beauty, time to go. I'll try and carry you if you want,' he said doubtfully.

I managed to rouse myself with a mental image of us collapsed on the pavement in a tangle of broken limbs. 'Sleeping Beauty was woken up by a kiss, as I recall.' I heard his soft laughter in the dark.

'I thought you'd never ask.'

He bent down over me and I felt shivers in the pit of my stomach. It was a very gentle kiss. 'I'll give you a call from Rome. Now you need to go to bed . . . sweet dreams, OK?'

I kept out of India's way over the next few days and tried not to think about the possible horrors of our trip to the film set on Friday. By now I didn't think that India had as much influence with Alex as she'd made out, but I knew she could still make life very difficult for me if she tried. Whenever I was tempted to tell her exactly what I thought of her pathetic scheming I remembered one of Alex's casual asides during our drive around Shoreditch: 'My kid sister's so pleased about you introducing her to Drake. It's great how the two of you get on – Indy's taken against a couple of my girlfriends in the past and it turned out she was dead right. She can be quite perceptive about people, you know . . .'

I was under no such illusions about India's powers of discernment or capacity for goodwill. It had taken her less than three minutes to notice my new necklace and only twenty seconds to write it off: 'Oh look, the Obelisk's got another of those sweet little pendant thingies. I keep telling Lex it would be *much* more practical to buy those necklaces in bulk since the silly boy gives so many of them away!' I didn't believe her, but she had still managed to take some of the shine off her brother's gift.

Dad was frantically busy, but he phoned late in the week to say that he'd forgotten to tell me they weren't in the studios on Friday but would be shooting on location. It was for a scene in a park, so they'd hired the grounds of a big Victorian mansion just outside London that they were also using for some interior scenes. They needed Drake for two scenes, one to be shot in the morning and the other later in the afternoon, so there should be plenty of time for introductions.

I said that this would be fine and communicated the news, together with instructions on how and when to get there, to India. She acted supremely bored by the whole thing. It was as if she had reluctantly been pressed into coming along and had only agreed to do so as a special favour to me. When I mentioned that Jess would be coming as well, India was full of helpful tips to set her at ease. 'What a *wonderful* treat for you! Now, try not to feel *too* intimidated, Jess. Drake must be *so* used to meeting people who feel overawed in a showbiz environment. It's all about positive reinforcement: keep telling yourself it's *possible* that you won't look as out of place as you feel.'

A typical day's filming started at eight and would go on for ten or eleven hours, but we weren't due to arrive until late morning, when Jess and I got a lift in from someone in the catering department. When we got there we found the mansion's drive filled with an organized chaos of trucks and trailers, including a paramedic's van and the cast and crew dining bus, a double-decker that also acted as a green room. There was also a small marquee where the extras (officially known as 'supporting actors') milled around holding polystyrene cups of coffee and looking bored. We went there first to meet the production secretary, Pip, who shook hands distractedly, thrust some visitors' badges at us, pointed us towards Dad and immediately dashed off muttering into her mobile phone. It seemed that we were going to be left to our own devices.

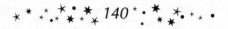

Although I've spent lots of time behind the scenes at various theatres and paid several visits to the American television studios where they make *Lady Jane,* it was a long time since I'd seen Dad at work on a film. Shooting on location is very different from filming in a studio, just as making a film is quite different from making a television series like *Lady Jane.* Most of *Lady Jane* is recorded before a live audience and nearly all the action takes place inside specially constructed sets – Lady Jane's apartment or her beauty salon or the coffee shop where she gets a disastrous waitressing job (in the series where her ex-husband cheats her out of her trust fund). Studio sets can be put up in a row like decorated boxes, with adjustable walls and ceilings to allow the camera team to move around. So although shooting on location is usually more authentic, I knew that it's often expensive and difficult. And shooting outside's the worst, because of unpredictable weather.

However, Friday morning was sunny and unseasonably warm, and seeing the orderly bustle around us I began to feel excited and optimistic in spite of myself; I looked at Jess and saw that she felt the same. We started to make our way over to the lawn where they were filming an 'intimate' discussion between Drake's character, Luke, and one of his supposed relatives, who's getting suspicious about Luke's background. Intimate, that is, apart from the producer, director, their assistants, the technical crew, photographers and publicists who were standing just a few feet away watching them. The lawn was meant to be in a wintry London park, so the design team had sprayed the whole area with fake frost (made of paper dust mixed with water), added a bench and a litter bin and installed some extras in the background to stroll about, play with dogs, push prams and so on. I was telling Jess how Dad's first ever film was set entirely in a park when India came sauntering across the drive towards us.

'My, my. Quite the Sunday-school outing, isn't it?' she said by way of greeting. 'This *is* going to be a cosy little threesome!' I'd half expected India to turn up in full Glamanatrix mode – towering heels, hair and bosom – but of course she was too smart to go for anything so obvious. She was wearing a figure-hugging black jersey dress under a scuffed red-leather jacket; her golden curls tumbled carelessly about her peachy-perfect face, her dark-blue eyes (Alex's eyes, I thought with a pang) looked out at us innocently from under long, sooty lashes. A single diamond on a thread of gold sparkled at her throat. I immediately thought how washed-out and drab I must look in comparison; I sensed Jess shift uncomfortably in her jeans and cotton jumper. India smiled sleekly and took us each by the arm. 'Shall we go and see the sights, then? . . . You know, Jess, I'd forgotten how very *ginger* your hair is. Once you get in the sun the orange bits are practically fluorescent!'

We continued our walk towards the camera, Jess and I with considerably less enthusiasm than before. Filming is more often than not a tedious and fiddly business and five seconds of screen time can require an hour of take upon take upon take. There are lots of different techniques and equipment you can use, but for this scene the camera was on a little truck that was pushed along a specially laid track, so that it could follow the actors as they moved along. Dialogue was picked up by the microphone, which was wielded from the end of the boom, a long pole attached to a tape recorder. Dad went over the scene with Drake and Polly, the actress playing the suspicious relative, while the focus puller prepared the camera for the shot. Then the clapper/loader loaded the film, put marks on the ground for the actors so they always hit the right spot during the scene and, when the camera was rolling, announced the scene and shot and banged the clapperboard so that sound and vision could be synchronized. Even the glamorous of stars acting from the most exciting of scripts can't make this process seem endlessly fascinating. However, the team seemed to be making good progress and they stopped for a lunch break well before we'd tired of watching.

After reading the *Venus* interview my expectations of Drake were not high, to say the least. I'm not sure *what* I expected, exactly, but if I hadn't known for sure that I was looking at the Real Drake Montague I don't think I would have recognized him. This isn't to say he wasn't as good-looking in the flesh – actually, he was better. *Much* better. Which was odd, because without the flattery of a camera's lens he wasn't nearly so picture-perfect: his skin not so glowing, his nose not so straight, his shoulders not quite so broad. He looked tired, too, with shadows under his eyes, and he was leaner, more edgy-looking, than I'd thought possible, all taut cheekbones and tawny hair. Most strikingly, the expression in those famously smoky eyes was intelligent and watchful. It was hard to believe that he'd not yet turned twenty. It was even harder to believe he was the same man as the pouting pretty-boy in the magazine.

The scene we were watching was a tricky one as the two characters were testing one another, trying to find out what the other was after; one moment they were playful, almost flirting, the next they were edgy and aggressive, only a step away from open confrontation. When Dad explained the kind of thing he wanted, Drake listened very closely. If he made a comment or query it was always quietly and intelligently put and, once he slipped into his role, the clutter of cameras and people around him seemed to fade away. I recognized the actress, Polly, as one of Dad's favourites; she'd been in several of his theatre productions and is a dark, intense-looking woman in her late twenties. However, I could see India looking her over with a satisfied air – she obviously thought that an old woman of nearly thirty couldn't be counted as competition.

When the group around the camera started packing up things and heading off towards the catering bus, Dad came over to us with Drake in tow. Dad looked tired but cheerful. 'Hello, girls, how nice to see you. I hope it's not been too dull for you – this project's a bit lacking in special effects and stunt action, I'm afraid. Drake, I'd like to introduce you to my daughter, Octavia, and two of her school friends, Jezabel and India.'

'Those are quite some names you've got there. Are all English girls so exotically christened, or is it just you three?' In spite of the shadows under his eyes, Drake's voice was full of warmth and energy and he grinned at us as he shook hands.

India simpered and tossed her head. 'India's where my father had his spiritual epiphany. Rich Withers, you know.'

'I guess it was lucky for you he didn't find God on Tooting Broadway,' said Drake. I hastily turned my snigger into a cough. 'Not that I'm one to talk. My agent chose my name for me – thought it sounded classy, and at the tender age of thirteen I didn't know any better.' We began strolling towards the catering bus. 'I was just desperate to escape the horror of Dwight Simpson.'

'That's your real name?'

'Yup. Nearly as ridiculous as Drake, isn't it?'

The afternoon had become so unexpectedly warm that we decided to turn lunch into a picnic. Dad likes a disciplined but informal atmosphere on set, with as little hierarchy as possible, so in the breaks between filming actors, extras and crew all mill around together. Drake had his own trailer, but he came to sit down with Dad and Polly and us, except that first Polly disappeared to answer her phone and then Dad was called away to sort something out with the location manager. It was odd to be sitting on the grass eating soup and sandwiches in the October sun, while just across from us was a wintry expanse of lawn and bare, frosted flower-beds. The feeling of unreality that comes of sharing sandwiches with a Hollywood film star soon wore off, however, as Drake was one of most easy-going people I've ever met. It was funny: he was better looking, richer and five hundred times more famous than Alex, and yet I didn't once feel intimidated in the way that I still sometimes did with Alex.

For one thing, Drake was so obviously impressed by my father. 'I was real worried I wouldn't be up to this part. At the beginning a lot of it was vanity, of course –

wanting to prove people wrong, wanting to avoid head-lines like "Montague told: Stick To The Day Job". Then once I started working with your dad I didn't care about the critics or the gossip columns in that way any more. I mean, I still care about the critics, but not on a *personal* level. I just don't want to let Hector and the rest of the guys here down. Because he took a risk in engaging me – sure, he's got some free publicity, but there's a whole heap of people hoping that we've both made a big mistake.'

I began to realize that Drake-the-heart-throb and Drake-the-actor were two very different people. I also saw how clever his answers had been in the *Venus* inter-view; how careful he'd been to say the things most people wanted and expected to hear while not giving anything personal away. 'Sooner or later,' he said, 'you have to make a choice as to whether you're going to walk away from the crowds and the lights and do your own thing or whether you're going to stay and play the game. Really smart people, *strong* people, are sometimes able to do both. I know I'm not like that. If I'm going to get free of all that so-called superstar crap I have to do it now or not at all. 'Cause before you know it, it's got too late.'

We were all silent after he said this. I, for one, was wondering what 'too late' actually meant. Your first session in rehab or your tenth? Or was it something as simple as not just wanting celebrity any more, but *needing* it? At any rate, I assured myself, Drake was talking about twenty-four-carat global stardom, not hanging around in a posh bar or two or trailing after your mother to a third-rate award ceremony. Anyway, I was different from the rest of the glamour junkies, Alex himself had said so. And Alex was soon going to be different too.

India had had quite enough of listening to us talk about Life Choices and the inspirational qualities of Hector Cleeve. She was sitting right opposite Drake, lounging in such a way that the clinging material of her dress had ridden high up her legs. She kept casually running her hands through her curls and then arching her neck to shake her hair free. Now she turned her back on Jess and me, leaned forward and locked eyes with Drake. 'Oh, God, I know. The burden of expectation on the modern artist is *intense*. My father always says that the role of the artist in society is to act as a sort of prophet, a sage . . . so one becomes a kind of . . . kind of . . . *divine spirit* to the masses. And then, of course, those who don't understand, those who *refuse* to understand, try to make up for their own *lack* – the *void* inside – by *sucking the life blood* from the true artist.'

Drake blinked. 'Well, you sure meet a lot of suckers in Hollywood.' India's face glowed with tender sympathy. Then she changed tack. Her voice became low and throbbing, she bit her lip and lowered her eyes bashfully.

'I know, Drake, what a *huge* fan you've become of the book they based this film on. I was reading *Gatherings* just the other day and it occurred to me how Murdochian your character is – the enigmatic figure who seems able to change the workings of destiny and all that. So I am just *so* excited to see how far the film will go in exploring the metaphysical dimension of the book . . . and of course it's your interpretation of the role that will really *elucidate* the enigma of Luke. I, well, I hardly know *anything* about this sort of thing, but it struck me that Luke's progress represents a . . . a *Platonic* journey of enlightenment. From material illusion to spiritual reality, you know.'

Drake scratched his head. 'I guess that's an, uh, interesting proposition. But what about chapter thirteen? It's obviously the crux of the book, and I think it causes a lot of problems for that theory. I mean, what do you think of Luke's behaviour towards Laura there?'

There was an expectant pause. For the first time in my life, I saw India looking uncertain, shifty even. She actually reddened. 'Well, I . . . it's . . . er . . .' We waited, but in vain. What's more, although Drake's expression was one of polite anticipation, I thought I detected the tiniest twitch of his lips. The kind of twitch your mouth makes when you're trying very hard to keep a straight face. It was then that the glorious realization dawned on me: *She hasn't even read the book.* She's just repeating some junk she read in a review or something. She hasn't got a clue – and Drake knows it.

Oddly enough, it was Jess who came to India's rescue. Jess hadn't said much over lunch but was sitting a little apart, tilting her face towards the sun, apparently lost in thought. I had, however, noticed Drake glancing over at her a couple of times. Now she turned to face us and pushed a coil of red hair from her face. 'Did you say that Luke was a Murdochian kind of figure?'

'So?' said India huffily. India being India, her moment of embarrassment had not lasted long. Now she was feeling vaguely wronged and there was an aggressive glint in her eye. 'What of it?'

'Oh, nothing really. It's just that I've been reading a Murdoch book lately . . . as usual, I didn't understand half the philosophical stuff, but it was really very good.'

'I've always thought him to be hugely overrated,' said India shortly. Drake broke in eagerly.

'You like Iris Murdoch too?' he asked Jess. 'Is this the first book of hers you've read? What's it called?'

India opened her mouth and shut it again. You could almost hear the snap. Jess settled herself more comfortably.

'Well, this one's a late one: *The Green Knight*. I started with *The Flight from the Enchanter,* because I liked the title, and then *Bruno's Dream,* which I didn't enjoy quite so much. And now this *Gatherings* man is supposed to be the "new Murdoch". But I don't want to start on the new one until I know the old one a bit better, you see.'

She smiled at us peacefully. The pale October sun had, as India had pointed out, intensified the colour of her hair. But it gleamed a really rich, golden-red, not ginger at all. She'd piled it up rather haphazardly and bound it in place with a turquoise scarf. I hadn't noticed before how green her eyes were. Come to think of it, I hadn't noticed what a great reader she was, either. Then I remembered all those times I'd found her with her nose in some book or other – she never mentioned what she was reading and I'd never bothered to ask, I realized uncomfortably.

Now she and Drake were in full flow, and not just about Iris Murdoch. It appeared that they had several literary enthusiasms in common.

'And have you read . . .'

'What do you think about . . .'

'All the reviews said . . .'

'The denouement . . .'

'Yes, but did you find . . .'

They only broke off when Drake had to go for his next scene. After he'd hurried off Jess looked after him with a little frown of concentration on her face. Then she caught my eye and raised her eyebrows impishly. There was a definite sparkle in her eyes, and I couldn't help grinning back. India had flounced off at the beginning of the 'And have you read?' conversation. Even from a distance I could see that she was now flirting outrageously with the publicist, the paramedic and a stray lighting technician.

It was late in the afternoon and long shadows had crept over the grass. Jess and I strolled over to watch some more filming; it was a different scene from the one shot in the morning and set in a different bit of the 'park'. A carefully choreographed bit of football was going on in the background, watched by Drake and the others. This time there was no frost and the actors weren't wrapped up in woollens as the action was supposed to be taking place a little earlier in the year.

Jess and I watched silently for a while, both of us, I guess, lost in our own thoughts. I was just about to announce that I was thinking of going and did she want to stay on or come back with me, when Drake broke away from the rest and hurried over to where we were standing.

'Hector said that you might be off now and I just wanted to say goodbye. I'm real pleased you came along.'

We both made the usual polite noises. He seemed to hesitate. 'Listen, after that talk we had . . . Iris Murdoch and all . . . I was wondering, there's this book reading, almost like a lecture, really, I'm going to try to fit it in somehow. The guy who wrote *Gatherings* is going to do it, so it's kinda like research for me. It's about his book but other people's work and ideas and philosophy stuff too. I don't suppose you'd like to give it a go?'

The invitation was addressed to both of us but it was Jess he was looking at. Feeling heroic, I said that I was unlikely to make it. 'Yes, I'd like that,' was all Jess said in her usual calm way, but she looked pleased, and so did Drake.

'Great. I'll be in touch. Gotta go now – bye, Jess, bye, Octavia, bye, er, India,' and he was gone.

We turned round to find that India had just come up behind us, a sneer on her face. But she didn't say anything, merely gave us a long stare, tossed her curls and stalked off down the drive. Jess suddenly looked stricken.

'Oh, God, Octavia. I should've *thought*. I've really, really messed things up with India and you, haven't I? And I was supposed to come along and make things easier, not *worse*. It's just that I – Drake – he . . . I didn't mean—'

'Don't worry – I'm not,' I assured her, not entirely sincerely. 'The only person who messed up today was India. And believe me, it was worth any amount of hassle just to see the look on her face when Drake asked her about chapter thirteen. That I will treasure until my dying day.'

'It was pretty wonderful, wasn't it?' Jess said with a giggle. Then she grimaced. 'Though I do wish she hadn't come up just when Drake invited us to that book thing. I know it's funny, and it serves her right . . . but she will be *mad*. At both of us.' I was inclined to agree, images of Marti Craddock and Desdemona Hughes and the rest of India's victims flashing before my eyes. But this wasn't the time to worry about it; I could see Jess's eyes were sparkling in spite of herself.

'No worries. The important thing is that India made a fool of herself and that you covered yourself in glory. Because it was blatantly obvious that Drake didn't ask "us" to the lecture. He asked *you*.'

If it had been me I'd have been hopping around and screeching like a maniac, but this wasn't Jess's style. It wasn't that she took the Darling approach, either. It's more a kind of *carefulness,* this calm, taking things slowly, making her mind up in her own precise, watchful way.

'Drake Montague,' she said wonderingly, as if trying out a new word. She shook her head and smiled. 'Wow.'

I didn't have much time between getting home and leaving for Viv's party. After the excitements and complications of the day, a big social event full of people I didn't know was the last thing I wanted, but I knew Viv would kill me if I tried to pull out. I checked my phone in the hope of finding a message from Alex to cheer me up, but I hadn't heard anything since he'd left for Rome on Tuesday. He was probably having too much fun with all those hot-blooded Latin lovelies to think of me, I thought grumpily as I ran my bath and foraged for supper.

Lady J. joined me in the kitchen as I was finishing off my cheese toastie. She was clearly torn between her time-honoured lack of interest in anything 'poor Hector' was involved in and a burning desire to get the latest Drake Montague gossip. She tried a few leading questions ('And how was your day, darling?'), but I wasn't about to let her off the hook, so made my answers as bland and unspecific as possible. Finally, curiosity won and she asked me straight out.

'Aren't you going to tell me what Drake was like, then?'

I thought for a moment. 'Clever. Quiet. Nice . . . not at all flashy. I think Dad's on to a winner.'

My mother pursed her lips. 'Hmph. He's terribly good-looking, I suppose? As handsome as he is on screen?'

'More handsome, as a matter of fact.'

'Ahh.' My mother was gratified. 'And did India and your other friend, er, Jessica, did they enjoy themselves?'

'*Jezabel* certainly did. She's going to a book reading or lecture or something with Drake . . . Did you know that his real name's Dwight Simpson?'

But my mother was not interested in Dwight Simpson. She was frowning. 'He's taking Jezabel? The ginger one? Not India? How very *odd* of him. And a book reading too! Though, honestly,' she said, drawing herself up, 'if he was going to take anyone anywhere, it really should be you. You're the one with the *connection*.'

'Ah, but maybe Alex wouldn't like it,' I said

mischievously. Lady Jane, however, looked thoughtful and nodded her head wisely.

'Yes, you're probably right. Men can be so *sensitive* about these things. But really . . . if it comes down to it . . . Alexis is super, of course, but if Drake, now . . . Jezabel *is* the ginger one, isn't she?'

I met up with Viv outside the tube station. She'd spent a fairly tedious 'Take Your Daughter to Work Day' at her father's bank and was raring to go. 'Fill me in quick, before we get there. How was it?'

'Disastrous. Fabulous.' I hardly knew myself. I sketched in the main events of the day, but Viv seemed most impressed by the revelation of Drake, the closet bookworm. She was highly sceptical to begin with.

'Are you *sure* it's the same guy as the one in *Psychlone*? The one who ran around smashing things up and grunting?' I assured her that this was the case. 'Wow,' she said, marvelling, 'Drake Montague can *read*! It's like finding out that Rich Withers likes to crochet in his spare time!'

She said this just as we arrived at the house where the party was taking place. I hung back a little, but then I remembered that I was no longer Dave, the Obelisk, but Octavia, consort to the Prince of A-listers, companion of movie stars, the girl who'd supplanted WeeWee and dazzled Nick. So I followed Viv into the crowded hallway as if I had every right to be there and every expectation of having a good time. It was a most peculiar feeling. Going out with Alex had made me a lot more confident about this sort of thing, I realized. It also occurred to me that knowing the evening was a Darling-free zone had released me from the kind of pressure that I'd almost come to accept was part of normal social activity.

I *did* have a good time. I didn't stick by Viv for all or even most of the night. I talked to lots of people, danced with a few and grew cheerful and chatty. It was easy to forget about India when surrounded by people who neither knew nor cared who she was. Afterwards, while we were waiting for the night bus, I told Viv what a good time I'd had and thanked her for making me come. She smiled and looked smug. 'You're so lucky, Viv. Your friends . . . the people from your school . . . they're so, well, normal. Fun and interesting and not always going on and on about their therapist or their modelling contract or how many times they appeared in *Prattler* last month . . . And really laid-back, too. Not stand-offish at all.'

'I guess you're right,' said Viv slowly. 'We – they – the people at school *are* a nice lot. On the whole. But that doesn't mean there aren't any horrors, either. We've still got bitchy beauty queens like India and sleazy creeps like Zack and gormless groupies like China and the rest. You can't get away from people like that. *They're* normal.'

On one level, I knew Viv was right, even though I still thought that Darlinham House was the kind of place where people like that are especially common and extra toxic. But when I mentioned this to Viv she turned to look at me in a serious sort of way.

'Be honest, now. Do you really, truly think that Alex is so different to the rest of the Darling crowd?'

'Yes, I do,' I said defiantly. 'He *respects* me because

I'm not superficial or frivolous like the rest of them. And he doesn't want people to think he's like that either. He told me he wants to change.' Well, not in those exact words, but I knew what he meant.

'He "wants to change"? Come on, girl – that's one of the cheesiest lines in the book. Downtrodden, deluded women have been falling for it for years.'

'Alex isn't a wife-beater or a drug addict, for God's sake.' I was getting irritated.

'No. He's a poor little rich boy who wants to be taken seriously.'

'And what's so wrong with that? Look, he's not perfect, I never expected him to be. But you haven't even met him yet and you're already casting judgement. Think about the sort of life he's had: the supermodel-super-bitch mum, the crazy rock-star dad, the ex-girlfriends from designer hell, the posh boarding school . . . it's a small miracle Alex hasn't turned out a monster like his sister. How can someone like you understand the kind of pressures he's had to deal with?'

Viv was staring at me. '*Someone like me?* Someone of the bog-standard, common-or-garden class, I presume.'

'God, Viv – I didn't mean that. I'm sorry, you know I don't—'

'No, don't apologize. You're right – I couldn't possibly begin to understand the trauma of growing up with all that horrible super-starry pampering.'

We waited in silence for the next few minutes. I could have kicked myself for spoiling the evening, but although I wanted to put things right again I wasn't quite sure how to start. However, when the bus finally wheezed towards us it was Viv who made the peace.

'You know what, if you say Alex is one of the good guys then I should take your word for it . . . and you're right, it *is* unfair to run him down before I've even met him.'

'I still shouldn't have gone all Lady Jane on you. I don't know what got into me.'

'Never mind that for now,' she said as she boarded the bus. 'It's agreed that Alex has taken the first step on the rocky road to social rehabilitation. But even so I think you should still be a little . . . careful. Just in case.'

Jess wasn't in school on Monday. India was, alas, and I arrived to hear her holding forth in the common room while the rest of the Darlings lounged on the black leather sofas, enjoying the first espressos and cigarettes of the day.

'. . . *Such* a disappointment. This is why one should never believe the hype about these people. Honestly – Drake Montague, an intellectual! I don't know whose idea it was, trying to promote him as some kind of hunk-with-brains, but it has *seriously* backfired. That kind of trick always does. And, you know, he's not even that good-looking. Not when you get up *close*. Actually,' she confided, lowering her voice, 'it was almost *embarrassing,* seeing him straining for effect like that. Trying to impress. I felt quite sorry for him. And for poor Hector Cleeve, of course. Both of them are quite obviously *out of their depth.*'

It was hard work trying to keep a straight face when I heard all this, but I reckoned my only hope of a peaceful start to the week was to keep out of India's way. Unfortunately, once India saw me, escape was impossible.

'Oh look – it's the Obelisk. Did you have a nice weekend, Davy? Lex is back now, as I'm *sure* you know. I'm sure he phoned you the *minute* he got back to tell you all about it. No? Strange . . . Well, he had an absolutely *fabulous* time, of course. Raffaella's been such a *devoted* friend of his for so many years. She's always up for *anything* – a real party animal, that girl. And how wonderful that LeeLee happened to be doing a shoot in Rome that same week . . . Goodness, you're looking just a teeny bit tense, Dave.' India's expression was brimming over with sisterly concern. 'Really, you've got *absolutely nothing* to worry about. I'm sure Lex and LeeLee's relationship is purely platonic, you know.'

This was an opportunity too good to miss. I widened my eyes innocently. 'Platonic? As in the just-good-friends meaning of the word? Or do you mean Platonic in terms of . . . what was it? . . . Oh yes. A journey of enlightenment. From material illusion to spiritual reality. Wasn't that how you put it the other day?'

China and Asia and Zack and the rest looked confused. But India actually went a little red. For once, just once, I'd managed to shut her up.

Neither Jess nor India turned up on Tuesday. I put this down to a fuzzy photograph on page two of the *Daily Bellower*, with a caption that read 'Montague Linked With Mystery Redhead'. The paragraph on page four of the *People's Snitch* announced that 'Drake Montague, smouldering hero of *High School Romeo* and this summer's smash hit *Psychlone*, has been spotted enjoying a night on the town in the company of a flame-haired siren, identity unknown.' We were informed that Drake was in London filming a 'hip new Brit-flick' to be directed by 'Hester Clive'.

Drake had photographed well, but the mystery redhead's features were very blurred, presumably because she'd moved just as the picture was taken. I thought I could make out a man standing at a reading-desk behind them. Clearly, the tabloids' definition of a night 'out on the town' was broadminded enough to include an hour or so in a lecture theatre.

I suppose Jess had got off lightly; Prince Richard's antics with a Lebanese belly dancer had taken up most of the headlines. Nevertheless by some mysterious means the identity of Drake's companion was common knowledge in Darlinham House. Darlings claim never to read newspapers (in keeping with their parents' attitude to the press – a delicate blend of anxiety, deference and contempt), but they always manage to be bang up to date with the latest crop of tabloid-column inches. Everyone, especially the girls, was determined to be spectacularly unimpressed, but without India to set the tone it was a bit of a struggle.

' "Flame-haired!" Ha! Everyone knows that's just a fancy way of saying ginger.'

'Maybe Drake's got, like, a *thing* for redheads. Some kind of weird *fetish*.'

'Creepy . . . Where were they, anyway? Didn't look like any bar I've ever been to.'

'The Obelisk probably knows,' said someone. 'She's

the one who took Jess along with India on Friday, after all.'

I shrugged. 'It's news to me.'

'Well,' said Asia with a determined air, 'I actually *pity* poor Jess. Didn't India say that Drake was a complete loser? And really ugly, too.'

But not everyone was convinced by this line of reasoning. Tallulah looked wistful. 'Even so . . . I can't help thinking . . . well, that I still wouldn't say no. To Drake, I mean.'

'You know, I've always thought that Jess could turn out to be a bit of a fox,' revealed Seth. 'She's got a certain look about her. Feisty.'

'It's always the quiet ones,' said Zack, with a leer in my direction.

All in all, it was a relief to escape Darlinham House for lunch with Alex (in spite of India's insinuations, he'd phoned on Monday night with apologies for not calling sooner). It was just over a week since we'd last seen each other and, despite the events of Friday, I was looking forward to it. The restaurant was in the premises of a private members' club in Bloomsbury and had a big, sunny dining room with floor-to-ceiling windows and black-and-white photos of style icons from the 1960s on the walls. However, lunch did not begin well. Alex appeared to still be hung over from the revelry of the past week; he had also come down with a cold, and this made him irritable.

'They're a hell of a lot less choosy about their clientele since I was last here,' he muttered to me, none too quietly, and with a contemptuous glance at two women who were just leaving; a plump, jolly-looking pair laden with shopping bags and talking loudly about the merits of rival dog-shampoo brands. We were waiting to be shown to our table, a delay that Alex seemed to regard as a personal affront. 'And the staff are apparently recruited from the Bonanza-Burger school of customer service. Hey, you. Yes, you. We've been waiting here for nearly ten minutes.'

'I'm extremely sorry, sir, but we're somewhat short-staffed at the mo—'

'I don't want excuses. I want *service*. Perhaps if you had a go at scraping plates instead of gliding around looking decorative we might actually get to sit down in the next hour.'

'I quite understand, sir. Now, if you'd like to follow me . . .' The waiter threaded his way through the room, his back held stiff with dislike. I tried to thank him but realized that I just sounded patronizing.

'Indy doesn't seem too pleased with you,' Alex announced when we'd finally been shown to a table that met with his satisfaction.

'Oh? What did she say?' Since *I* wasn't too pleased with Alex at the moment I found it hard to strike the appropriate note of concern. In fact, I sounded distinctly frosty, but Alex seemed oblivious to the chill settling over our particular corner of the restaurant.

'Oh . . . you know what she's like. Nothing much . . . probably just PMT . . . For Christ's sake, this glass is *warm*. Those morons must have just taken it out of the dishwasher! Feel it.' I felt it. It was, indeed, ever so slightly warm to the touch. 'They can't seriously expect me to drink white wine out of this . . .' He summoned our long-suffering waiter and demanded a new, cool wine glass. And the adjustment of the shutter because the light from the window was making him squint. And a different bottle of mineral water because this brand left an aftertaste. By this time our fellow diners were telegraphing their disapproval with raised eyebrows and meaningful looks. I felt my cheeks go hot with embarrassment but felt that creating a further scene between Alex and me would hardly improve matters. If I kicked him under the table he'd probably blame a faulty table-leg and sue the restaurant.

'How much do you hang out with India, anyway?' he asked.

'Uh, well. It's a small class. We all kind of stick together,' I said evasively.

'Yes, but who do you spend time with *particularly*? Who are the people you like to be seen with?' He was leaning forward intently.

'Like to be *seen with*?' I stared at him. 'What happened to the principle of just being around people you like? Who you want to know better? Skeletons in closets, warts and all, remember?'

'Oh . . . yeah.' Alex frowned, then pulled a face and smiled awkwardly. 'Hell, I'm really sorry, Octavia. I know I can be a God-awful brat sometimes. All that throwing my weight around is just showing off, you know. Probably some sort of raging inferiority complex.' He squeezed my hand and looked at me rather anxiously. 'I'm feeling crap, but that's no excuse.'

After that, things were better. The food was excellent; Alex only played around with a salad, but I had a fantastic wild venison fricassée followed by a brandy and apricot cheesecake. Alex watched my progression through the meal with interest.

'You're the first girl I've ever taken out who's eaten like this.'

'Eaten like what?' I asked suspiciously, fork laden with cheesecake hovering in the air.

'Well, like a bloke. Don't worry,' he added hastily, 'I think it's kind of cute . . . Actually, Raffaella eats like you do. Only she goes off and makes herself throw it all up at the end.' I looked to check he was joking but couldn't quite tell. However, the mention of Raffaella put me in mind of something that had been nagging me.

'Did W— LeeLee enjoy Rome?'

'What?' Was it my imagination, or was Alex suddenly looking shifty?

'LeeLee. India mentioned that she was out in Italy. With you.' I was careful to sound unconcerned. Friendly interest, that was all.

'Oh. Right. Er, yeah, LeeLee's fine. Working hard.'

Poor WeeWee, I thought, all that lounging around in Rome, modelling designer dresses while people tell you what a goddess you are . . . must be tough.

But I changed the subject, and we both finished the meal in a more cheerful mood than we'd begun it in. Alex said he'd better go home and nurse his cold for a couple of days, but would get in touch ASAP. 'You really should have come to Rome,' he said as we parted, 'it would have been wild.' I didn't remind him that he hadn't actually invited me.

*

Although I'd enjoyed lunch, it had left me with a feeling of unease. It was partly because of Alex's reaction to my mentioning WeeWee, but also because of how the waiter had looked at us as we left the restaurant – *just another pair of spoilt rich kids,* was what he was thinking. Alex had apologized to me for acting like a 'God-awful brat', and I'd believed he meant it; now and again he'd come out with some self-mocking remark or other, some flash of self-knowledge, which made me feel a rush of warmth, of tenderness, towards him. Yet this didn't alter the fact that he'd been carelessly, confidently rude to everyone who'd attended us in the restaurant, almost without being aware of it. I thought of lunch with Drake Montague, sitting on the grass and eating sandwiches from the canteen bus. *Sooner or later,* he'd said, *you have to make a choice.*

I'd have liked to talk all this over with Viv, but I knew exactly what her reaction would be. What else did I expect? Alex was just an immature, arrogant chauvinist who didn't deserve me. Or anyone else, for that matter. My mother, equally predictably, would babble on about what a charming, attractive young man everybody knew Alexis was, and being the son of Rich Withers one might expect him to be just a *little* tempestuous but, really, you wouldn't want him to be too nice because that could get a touch, well, boring. Since Friday, the only conversation Dad had had time for was a three-minute chat to thank him for letting us watch the filming. I could phone Jess, I supposed . . . but it was too soon after her appearance in the gossip columns, and I didn't want her to think I was only calling to get the dirt on Drake. No wonder she was lying low; if it was me I would have put off facing the envious resentment of India and Co. for as long as possible. However, just as I'd decided to call Michael for a chat about unimportant, pleasant things such as the colour scheme for the dining room, Jess telephoned me herself. It was officially to ask about the work she'd missed at school, but she came to the real point soon enough.

After I assured her that the powers-that-be at Darlinham House had not yet remarked upon (or noticed) her absence, she asked if India had been in school. I told her that India was almost certainly sulking at home after the photo in the papers. There was a pause; I wasn't quite sure if Jess wanted me to ask her about Drake or not. 'Ah. I suppose the Darlings saw it too?'

'Yup. Asia, China and Cleopatra are terribly sorry for you. Twinkle and Tallulah are not so sure. Oh, and Seth reckons he's always suspected you of being a secret sex fiend.'

Jess laughed. 'So I can safely expect to be ignored as usual once I get back?' I assured her that no one was going to lower their dignity by showing any signs of interest in her or Drake's private lives.

'How was it, anyway?' I finally asked.

'Oh, it was really nice. The man doing the lecture – you know, the one who wrote *Gatherings* – well, we were a bit worried at first because he started off sort of twitchy and mumbling. But once he got into the swing of things it was *fantastic* – time for questions at the end and everything . . . Drake's met him before and so he got a signed copy of the book for me. We went out for pizza afterwards. Drake had to wear this weird shaggy wig as a disguise.'

'So Drake was, er, nice?'

'Well, you know what he's like. Really friendly.'

'Just friendly?' I couldn't stop myself asking.

'Yes, just friendly.' Jess sounded both relaxed and amused. 'It turns out that we've got loads of things in common – like and dislikes, that is. It's not as if our lifestyles are at all similar. So we just talked and talked. Drake hasn't got much free time and of course he's going back to the States soon. But we're going to try and get to the theatre some time next week.'

'Great,' I said weakly. How could Jess be so unfussed about all this? So easy-going? Maybe I was just the emotional, neurotic type – the kind of person who saw complications and crises everywhere.

'And I wanted to thank you again. For Friday and everything; I know it wasn't what you'd planned exactly . . . how are things with you and Alex, anyway?'

'Oh, fine,' I said breezily. I crossed my fingers. 'Just fine.'

I'd been feeling a little sorry for myself all week, so on Friday I came back from school determined to spend an evening slumped in front of the television, painting my toenails and alternating between a jumbo pack of salt 'n vinegar crisps and yogurt-coated banana chips. The ultimate slob therapy. However, just as I was settling down to some kiddie cartoons the doorbell to the flat rang. It was Alex.

'Hi.'

'Hi.'

We both looked a bit taken aback to see each other – me because Alex was the last person I expected (or wanted) to see prior to an evening of coach-potato bliss; Alex, presumably, because the sight of me in ancient T-shirt and baggy trousers with banana-chip crumbs around my mouth was something of a revelation. After all, Alex had only ever seen me after careful grooming sessions involving lipgloss, stage-managed hair and Lady Jane's wardrobe revolution.

'Somebody let me in the main entrance,' he said by way of explanation, eyebrow raised. 'You look very . . . relaxed. Have I come at a bad time?'

'I guess I'll have to cancel my threesome with Scooby Doo and the Irish chap from *Blue Peter*. Other than that, come on in.' I led the way into the living room, brushing crumbs from my T-shirt and uttering a silent prayer of thanks that I'd not yet had the chance to move into my purple tracksuit bottoms and novelty poodle slippers. 'How's the cold, anyway?'

'Nearly gone. I was going mad stuck at home with just me and the Filipinas, though. So I thought I'd come and pay you a visit.' Alex looked around him with interest. 'The last few times I've been in your neigh- bourhood it's been the dead of night . . . Dad used to have a place just down the road, you know. A proper house, obviously, not a flat.'

'*Obviously*,' I said under my breath. I should have remembered that no true rock star would be satisfied with anything less than an eight-bedroomed mansion and an army of Filipina chambermaids. Alex was walk- ing around the room, looking pictures up and down, running a finger along the furniture, eyeing up Lady J.'s flower arrangement. Our flat's not particularly large, but it's part of a big, posh nineteenth-century town house and, as you'd expect, my mother's been very careful to 'strike the right note', as she puts it. It's all very plush, very tasteful, very Lady Jane, I suppose. Alex picked up a little porcelain figurine of a shepherdess. He turned it round in his hands speculatively, not really looking at it; then he brushed a speck of dust from her skirt and replaced the figurine on the mantelpiece, shifting it about until he was satisfied with its new position.

I know how that shepherdess feels, I suddenly thought. Tweaked and polished and pointlessly rearranged. Then I considered that this wasn't fair – any adjustment to my way of doing things had been up to me, hadn't it? *I* was the one prepared to turn myself into what everyone else wanted me to be. Nobody had put a gun to my head and forced me to start wearing lipgloss.

Now Alex was examining our framed photographs. He picked one up. 'I didn't know you had a big sister, Octavia. Quite a cutie.'

'It's my mother,' I said coldly. I don't like that photo, even though it was only taken last year. My mother and I are on a beach, there's a breeze, and my mother's just got hold of me round the waist. Her hair is blowing everywhere and she's laughing. I'm smiling for the camera but I'm not looking entirely comfortable. I'm not really a beach person. My mother is.

'Oh,' said Alex, 'of course. She's got a part in some sitcom, hasn't she?'

Now, for some reason, I was feeling defensive. 'She's the lead, actually. It's American and it's been going for years. It's very popular.'

'That's quite a coincidence – as a matter of fact, I'm a bit of a Clairbrook-Cleeve fan myself.' He smiled over at me and I couldn't help smiling back.

'Really? What's the basis of the attraction?'

'Maybe you should come over here and remind me.'

I went over and kissed him. 'Hmm. Yes, that's definitely part of the appeal . . . but I think I might need to explore this further. Make a proper analysis. I wouldn't want you thinking I'm just another mindless groupie.'

His analysis progressed so satisfactorily that we moved to the couch. We hadn't been there very long when Alex, shifting about, pulled out a cushion from under him only to find that it was in fact one half of my pink poodle slippers. Strictly speaking, they're more grey than pink, and this one was missing an ear. I think it might even have had a banana chip clinging to its underside.

'This yours?'

'It belongs to the butler, actually.' I put it and its brother on my feet and waggled them defiantly. Alex looked from my slippers to me with an extremely bemused expression.

'Have you got any other wardrobe secrets I should know about?'

'Oooh, a whole closet full of skeletons, I should think. But don't fret,' I said acidly, 'they're designed according to the very latest model.'

He was quiet for a few moments. 'I think poodles beat skeletons in the style-stakes hands down.' He took hold of my hand. 'You know, Octavia, I can never tell what you're thinking. Sometimes I'm not even sure how much . . . well, I'm not always sure what you think of me.' If only I knew, I thought to myself and smiled, rather ruefully. Alex caught my smile.

'That's exactly what I mean, Mystery Girl. Come here . . .' He kissed me softly, and I felt a familiar rush of longing and sweetness and uncertainty. 'Don't give up on me just yet.' I nestled my head into his arm and we sat there quietly, Alex stroking my hair.

'Octavia?'

'Mmmm?'

'Have you ever thought about going blonde?'

I froze. About a hundred and one exclamations were struggling in my throat, none of them printable. '*What—*'

There was the sound of a key in the door.

'Oh, goodness. Oh – I do hope I'm not interrupting . . .' My mother was fluttering at the entrance to the living room. 'I'm sorry, Octavia. I didn't know you were expecting a guest.' She was smoothing her hair and smiling shyly – wasn't *I* the one who was supposed to be embarrassed here? Alex got up at once and went to shake hands, princely charm radiating from every pore.

'It's I who should be apologizing, Mrs Clairbrook-Cleeve. I'm afraid I've barged in uninvited this evening. I'm Alex. So pleased to meet you.'

'Oh, call me Helena, please.' My mother actually blushed. 'And it's always such a treat meeting Octavia's friends. We all lead such busy lives these days . . . people never have enough time to be introduced *properly* . . . But I expect I'm just being old-fashioned.'

'I find that extremely hard to believe.' Alex's tone was pitched just the right side of smarmy. I thought of

India, switching on the sweetness in a bat of the eye. Lady Jane was still a little pink.

'Well, in any case, I do hope you'll be staying at least for a drink? As you can see, it's going to be a very *informal* evening . . .' She shot me a meaningful look. I stuck my hands in the pockets of my rumpled trousers defiantly. My mother, of course, looked impeccable in a clinging rose-coloured sheath dress.

Off she went to get the drinks. Alex, to my irritation, was supremely relaxed, sprawled all over the chaise longue and grinning to himself at some private joke. I was desperate to ask him exactly what he'd meant by the blonde remark, but it was impossible with Lady Jane floating around the place. 'What are you smirking at?' I asked.

'You,' came the unwelcome reply. 'Standing there glowering in those funny clothes. While your mother—' But I never heard what was so amusing/interesting about my mother, since at that moment she returned with a tray of glasses and ice cubes and things.

She and Alex were soon sitting facing each other and merrily chatting away, Alex dredging up vague and probably fraudulent childhood memories of living in our street, my mother reminiscing about the time Tigerlily Clements had 'nearly' guest-starred on *Lady Jane*. I realized that if I wasn't going to be completely excluded from things I'd better abandon the glower and start nodding and smiling in the right places. I even took the opportunity of fetching more tonic water to go and change into a pair of fairly respectable black trousers. When I got back, I found my mother, bright-eyed and talking animatedly, leaning across the coffee table to top up Alex's glass. And Alex was staring at the low neck of her dress, right down her cleavage.

Lady Jane was blissfully aware of the appreciative focus of Alex's gaze, but there was no way she could avoid the next super-strength glare I gave her. Perhaps it was just as well she interpreted it as a strategic hint.

'Well, I don't want to be in your way,' she said, smiling fondly at the two of us. She checked her watch. 'Goodness – I'm going to be *wildly* late . . . I was meant to be at Toto and Tiara's twenty minutes ago! I'll see you in the morning, Octavia, darling. Goodbye, Alexis – Alex, I mean.' Kiss, kiss. 'I've *so* enjoyed our chat.'

Alex, ever the gentleman, opened the door for her as she left the room. 'Sweet,' was his only comment.

I, meanwhile, was taking deep breaths and counting slowly up to ten. It's OK, I told myself very coolly and calmly, it doesn't mean anything. It's just a general male breast fixation. I sat down next to Alex and forced myself to speak normally, even though I felt that my voice was about to crack into a hundred little pieces. 'Alex . . . do you think I look like my mother? At all?'

If he was surprised by my question he didn't show it. 'Maybe a bit,' he said, considering. 'Around the chin. Kind of determined looking. And your lips are shaped the same.'

What was he doing looking at my mother's lips? A wave of jealous rage and misery shook me, and I found I was trembling.

'Look, are you OK, Octavia? You're not coming down with my cold, are you? You seem a bit out of sorts tonight.' He sounded concerned but also slightly impatient. How could he not realize what was wrong? I wanted to kick him, hard, but I also wanted to *kiss* him. I wanted him to sweep me into his manly arms while he murmured, 'You are the only one for me, my wonderful, special, incomparable Octavia.' But most of all I wanted to be alone. I needed to be rid of both of them. I dug my nails hard into my palm, using the pain to steady me.

'Sorry,' I said, forcing a smile. 'I think you may be right. I haven't really been feeling myself all day. Probably the beginnings of a cold.'

'Hmm, yes, you're looking rather white. Poor old you. Well, I'll leave you in peace to recuperate – I know what it's like when you're feeling crap. Have an early night and I'll see you tomorrow. Oh, and thank your mother for the drinks again, will you?'

He kissed me on the cheek and went out of the door, whistling.

I hardly slept at all that night. Immediately after Alex left I wished I'd held my nerve and confronted him there and then. I went over and over every detail of his visit until every remark he made, every look he gave, had some insulting implication. Stupid, shallow, insensitive git. But who was I angrier with anyway, Alex or Lady Jane? I thought about staying up until my mother got back and having it out with her instead, but I didn't know exactly what I'd be accusing her of. It wasn't that I really believed my mother was trying to seduce my boyfriend; the thing was, she'd behaved the same way around Alex as she did around everyone else – the same old sweet, ditzy, glitzy Helena. My mother the Prom Queen. Who was probably congratulating herself even now on what a wonderful job she'd made of setting us all at ease. My mother the Gracious Hostess. I ground my teeth.

Then I started to wonder if I was being paranoid and hysterical. Maybe the whole ogling-my-mother thing was something I should just be able to laugh off. Maybe it was all a natural consequence of what Viv referred to, pityingly, as the Ape-Man Lechery Gene. But I don't mind Alex being lecherous, I reasoned with myself, burying my head deep under my pillow. I just want him to reserve his lechery for *me* – even though I'll never be a pygmy blonde and won't ever be asked to present an award or launch a perfume. Even though I'll always prefer to wear grubby slippers rather than sparkly heels . . . I felt tears of self-pity prick my eyes and turned over in bed for what felt like the hundred and fiftieth time that night.

The next morning I felt better, as you always do. I picked up the heart necklace from the floor where I'd thrown it last night and stood turning it over in my hands for a while. *Don't give up on me*, he'd said. I was less angry with Alex, but also less sure of my own feelings. Was this about Alex and my mother, or Alex and me? Was it simply a case of injured pride, because the gentleman expressed a preference for blondes? Or was the real problem something else, something that had been building up over time and that I didn't want to admit to – something to do with the porcelain shepherdess, something mixed up with LeeLee and my mother and Drake? It all kept going round and round and round in my head – not only the night before, but everything that had happened since I received my invitation to India's party.

I needed to talk to Viv. She might say 'I told you so', but I knew she wouldn't fuss or gush over me. I needed her ruthlessness; I needed to be forced into deciding once and for all exactly what I wanted and why.

But that morning, just as I was leaving the house to go to Viv's, Alex himself drove up in his sleek black convertible. Although it was a dull November day he'd put the hood down and was wearing sunglasses. He pulled up at an angle on the pavement outside our building and left the engine running – he was just off to meet his mother for lunch and was already late.

'How you feeling?'

'Better, thanks, but I—'

'That's great. I'll take you out tonight to celebrate. Look, I'm in a rush but I thought I'd come by to tell you about Friday before I forget.'

'Friday?'

'Yeah. I won't be around much this week. Mum's in town for her annual mother-son bonding trip. But on Friday night I've got us an invite to the Quicksilver Global Music Awards. There's going to be one hell of a party afterwards, so you'll have to get something to wear, OK?' He was about to drive off.

I took a deep, steadying breath and clenched my hands inside my pockets. 'Alex, wait – I need to talk to you. It's important.'

'God, Octavia, can't it wait? I'm already late. Look, if you're worried about finding the right sort of outfit, have a word with Indy. She's a pro at the whole shopping thing.'

I almost laughed in spite of myself. 'Is that your definition of important? Finding the right sort of frock for a party? Dying my hair the right shade of blonde?'

'Am I missing something here?' At least he cut the ignition and actually looked at me, albeit in a long-suffering sort of way.

'Just for a start, you haven't even asked me if I'm going to be free on Friday.'

He sighed an exaggeratedly patient sigh. 'Well, aren't you?'

'As a matter of fact, I'm not,' I said crisply. 'It's Michael's birthday on Friday. We're going out. It's been arranged for ages.'

'Michael?' Alex frowned.

'Dad's boyfriend.'

'Oh. Well, you can certainly miss *that*.'

'No, Alex, I can't.'

'Sure you can,' he said, drumming his fingers on the wheel impatiently. 'Look, Octavia, I don't want you to take this the wrong way, but sometimes your priorities can be a little off. Friday is a *big* deal and so are all the people associated with it. It's a *global event*, for Christ's sake. The press will be all over the place.'

'That's not the point,' I said very quietly.

'Isn't it? Indy was saying only the other day that you're a bit . . . funny . . . a bit offhand about this kind of thing. Sure, there's nothing worse than being seen as trying too hard. I am *completely* with you there. It's one of the reasons I like you, because you keep your own distance. I've told you that. But even so, you've still got to . . .' he searched for the right words '. . . pay attention to how the scene operates. How to keep on the circuit. OK, so your parents might not be major-league players (though if this Drake Montague project comes off, that might change), but the connections are there. You're part of this world. You just need to work at it a little.'

I took a step back from the car. I felt oddly light-hearted. Of course I didn't need Viv or anyone else to tell me what I wanted or what to do; it was very simple, perhaps I'd known the answer all along. Alex might want to be taken seriously, but he didn't want to change, not really. Because he didn't just want the glitz and the glamour – he *needed* it. He needed the attention but also the security, the self-assurance it gave.

'I understand. But I still can't come on Friday.'

'Jesus, Octavia . . . look, I've got to go. We'll talk about this tonight.'

'I can't do tonight either.'

'*What?*'

'I'm sorry, Alex. I just can't do it.' I took another step back from the car, knowing as I did so that we both understood what I meant by it. Last night I had imagined this moment as one of high drama, of confrontation and tears and recrimination. At that time it was still only a possibility, unreal and exaggerated like a scene from a bad soap opera. I guess part of me had been secretly hoping that Alex would have an overnight conversion, that he would charge into the flat and fall at my feet, pleading with me to give him one last chance now he could see the error of his selfish and shallow ways. Now I didn't feel any of the anger or hurt of the night before, only a kind of calm. The last rush of longing and sweetness and uncertainty had gone. 'I don't think we'll ever want the same things, you see,' I said, with just the tiniest hint of regret.

We looked at each other for a long moment. Alex's expression was puzzled and also curious, and reminded me of the first time we met – how he looked at me like he was trying to work something out. I almost thought I saw a flicker of envy in his eyes. Then he sneered and all of a sudden it was like looking at India.

'Right. Fine. *Whatever,* Octavia.' And he roared off in that big black car with a great squeal of tyres. Exit Mr Wrong. It was just like the climax of a bad soap opera after all.

I turned round and went back very slowly into our building and very slowly climbed the stairs up to the flat. Lady Jane met me at the door. She'd been in bed for most of the morning and had only this minute emerged from the bathroom, perfectly dressed and made-up. Even the air around her smelt expensive.

'Darling! Was that Alexis who just drove off? Goodness, he did *tear* round that corner – was he in a frightful rush? Because if not, you really should have invited him in. It's nearly lunchtime, you know.'

'He wasn't hungry.' I tried to get past her into my bedroom.

'Did you actually *ask* him, Octavia?'

'It wasn't a good time.'

'Well, honestly! Keeping him waiting on the street like that! I know it's none of my business, but I do think the least the poor boy could expect was a little *graciousness* from you. You really were *very* offhand last night I thought. Those awful clothes, for one thing – I thought they'd gone to the charity shop long ago. And he's such a charming young man . . . especially when you consider what his father was like at that age.' She drew breath – it was obviously my morning for lectures. 'It's no use scowling like that, darling. Sometimes I don't think you appreciate how important it is to make an *effort* with these things. It's all about *paying attention* to people. You can't just expect everything to always fall into place for you. You have to work at—'

At this point I snapped.

'You see? You see?' I shouted, appealing to no one in particular. 'This is *exactly* what I mean! You're both as bad as each other!'

'Darling! What do you mean?'

'You really don't get it, do you?'

My mother looked tragic. 'Has something happened between the two of you? Oh, sweetheart, has Alex decided—'

'*Alex* hasn't decided anything. I know you think that he's out of my league and I'm eating my heart out because I just can't cut it in the A-list. Well, maybe I can't. But has it ever occurred to you that maybe I don't *want* to?'

'I thought – you – I wanted – we *did* talk about this. After the award ceremony. I thought you decided . . . otherwise I would never, ever, have tried to . . . to . . .' She seemed genuinely shocked. 'I know you don't find it easy but—'

'Easy? Well, you obviously find it *extremely* easy. Wearing tight dresses, fluttering your eyelashes, knocking back the bubbly . . . Maybe *you* should try going out with Alex. I'm sure the two of you would make a lovely couple. *Stellar!* could do a double-page celebrity profile.'

Her face had gone white. 'I only wanted to make

things right for you. I thought I was helping. Please believe me. Please.'

All the frustration and misery of the last night had come flooding back. 'No. You're only making things right for you. For what you want, not for me. And I hate it.' My voice rose and cracked. 'It's all such a *fake*! Looking right! Saying the right things! Meeting the right people! All you people think you're so bloody fabulous, sucking up to each other all the bloody time, sneering at everyone else, when actually it's *pathetic*! A pretentious, pathetic FAKE!' And I stormed into my room and slammed the door with the dramatic gesture of someone who knows the minute they stop shouting they're going to cry.

Over the next few days my mother and I went out of our way to avoid each other, and when our paths did cross we were excessively polite. She was much more quiet than usual and sometimes I caught her looking at me apprehensively, as if she was about to say something, but neither of us made any reference to my outburst, each retreating into a kind of nervous formality. After I'd fumed on the phone to Viv for a while, I calmed down enough to admit that maybe I'd taken a lot of my hurt and disappointment with Alex out on my mother. I remembered uneasily the shocked, white look on her face as I'd slammed the door. But I still blamed her for not seeing things as they really were, for not seeing *me*, for trying to make me into the kind of girl Alex wanted. The kind of daughter *she* wanted. A horrible sort of Tammy-India hybrid . . . I'd almost let myself believe her and pretend I could fit in with girls like that and be myself, too. Part of me still wanted to believe her, even now, and this I couldn't quite forgive.

I thought Viv would see my break up with Alex as cause for celebration rather than commiseration, but she sensed that I didn't want to talk about it much and just said that she was sorry. 'Maybe he just needs to grow up some more. Then one day he'll get tired of being an international playboy,' she suggested, only half joking, 'and camp out on your doorstep, begging for one last chance of social rehabilitation.' He didn't, of course, but, somewhat to my surprise, he didn't tell India about our split either.

I was absolutely convinced when I trailed dismally into school on Monday that she would be ready and waiting to start the gloat-fest. '*Poor* Dave,' she'd coo, 'I do hope he broke the news to you *gently* . . .' I was tempted to give myself the day off. Or maybe the rest of the term, come to think of it. Unfortunately, I knew she'd attribute this to the fact I was prostrate with grief after her handsome, heartbreaking, irresistible brother had dumped me. The possibility that he would tell her, or she would believe, that it had been the other way round was about as likely as Rich Withers becoming the Dalai Lama on his next trip to Tibet.

However, India appeared to be uninformed of the happy news and ignored me as usual. Indeed, she seemed rather distracted by something – disappearing for large parts of the school day and looking extra-specially smug in a secretive sort of way. She also spent a lot of time flirting and giggling and whispering with Cosmo, while Calypso looked haughty and aggrieved. I assumed some kind of love triangle was going on and hoped it would provide enough distraction to let my break up with Alex pass by relatively unremarked upon. I told Jess, but in a casual, just-in-passing sort of way, as if it wasn't a big deal. I felt a little shy of Jess just now. I gathered that the theatre trip with Drake had been a success, and although I reckoned she would tell me more about him if I asked her, she didn't volunteer anything and I felt she preferred it that way. She was her usual peaceful self, but that glazed, dazed look she sometimes wore was gone. A certain tilt to her chin, a certain brightness in her eye kept the pygmy blondes at bay.

Although I'd been spared India's triumph I knew this reprieve was only temporary. In fact, it was probably a ploy to lull me into a false sense of security while she found me the perfect punishment for her humiliation with Drake . . . Now that I didn't have Alex to distract me, the fallout from our little trip to the film set was beginning to prey on my mind. So perhaps it would be just as well if she thought that her precious Lex had dumped me. That way, I thought hopefully, India might think that the status quo had been restored and family honour satisfied.

All in all, it was a fairly miserable week. Ordinarily, I'd have been really looking forward to Michael's birthday dinner on Friday, but as I got ready to go out I couldn't stop myself thinking how different it would be if I was putting on a glittering evening gown, ready to be squired by Alex and to go guzzling vodka martinis with the A-list. Somehow the bright lights and red-carpet treatment looked a lot more attractive now that I'd given it up. I wondered whom Alex was taking instead of me – WeeWee? Raffaella? – and wondered if he thought about me at all.

I tried my best to shake off these pointless and self-pitying thoughts once I got to the restaurant where the birthday dinner was taking place. It was a small, select gathering and I knew most of the people there. There was lots of laughter and energetic talk and scandalous gossip about goings-on in both the theatrical and legal worlds. The food was fantastic too, and Michael looked very handsome and happy in the new jade silk shirt Dad had given him. I thought I'd made a good job of pretending to be as cheerful as everybody else, but as we were all taking a midnight stroll along the Embankment Dad dropped away from the group in front to ask me what was wrong.

'Your mother telephoned me last night, you know.' That meant it was serious: Lady Jane avoided consultations with 'poor Hector' where at all possible. 'She's worried about you.'

'I'm all right.'

'Are you? Look, she said something about a break up with this boy you've been seeing. Alex. I don't know what went on between you and him or the rights and wrongs of it, but you're entitled to stamp your feet and tear your hair out if you want to. Neither your mother nor I expect the saintly stiff upper lip—'

'It's not just about Alex,' I interrupted, 'and incredible as this may sound, *I* was the one who ended it. My mother is now having to come to terms with the fact that I'll never be the kind of girl who can lounge around in posh frocks in posh bars getting chatted up by the sons of superstars. I'm sorry if she's losing beauty sleep over it, but I'm sure she'll get over the disappointment eventually.'

'Listen. No, listen to me, Octavia. Sentimental as it may sound, the only thing your mother wants you to "be" is happy. People are difficult to work out, sometimes. What we wish for or think we want to be, what we need . . . it changes.'

I thought of all the moments when I'd felt uncertain about what I was doing or what I wanted, and how my mother had always steamrollered over these misgivings before I was even fully aware of them. *Don't be ridiculous. Nonsense. Silly Girl.* How she'd been there every step of the way, nagging and nudging and meddling so I could live up to her and Alex's lofty standards. I might not even have gone to India's wretched party if it wasn't for her.

'Maybe she'd have known what I wanted if she'd spent more time being my parent and less time acting like my publicist.'

As soon as I said it I regretted it. He stopped and faced me. 'Octavia. That is unfair and you know it. More than that, it's a very cruel thing to say.'

'I'm sorry. I'm sorry. I really am. It's just that . . .' To my shame I was getting tearful. I had to take a deep breath before I went on. 'I know it's my fault. I didn't want to think about the problems, not really, because I *did* want Alex. I did want glamour and posh parties and the rest of it, at least in the beginning. I wanted to – well, to *dazzle*, I suppose. And then I thought that Alex was different from the rest and perhaps we could – we could get away from it all. But it's so easy for Mum . . .

she's not like me, she's always known what she wants and how to get it. She looks the part, she's always so perfect . . .'

Dad had his arm around me by now and I was sniffling a bit. He stroked my hair. 'Your mother is very proud of you. We both are. And not just because you "dazzle" – you do, you know – but because you're intelligent and independent and brave.' He sighed. 'I don't think that it's always been easy for your mother. You never got to know her parents . . . but, well, let's just say they made disapproval into a full-time leisure activity. It was a very brave thing she did, coming to London so young, with nowhere to go, no one she knew. Then there was me and, ah, we all know how that turned out. She's had to work bloody hard to get where she is.'

'Right. Newcastle's own Eliza Doolittle.'

Dad laughed ruefully. 'I'm afraid I didn't make a very good Professor Higgins.' Then he was serious again. 'She did it all by herself, you know. I admire her.' We were both quiet for a few minutes, leaning over the wall to watch the Thames reflecting back the city's lights in spangles of gold. 'I don't think this is simply about Alex any more. Do you think, Octavia, you could sit down and explain everything to your mother? Where you want to go from here, what you want from your life? Telling her what you *don't* want is only the start, after all. I think you'll find she's ready to listen.'

I squeezed his hand to show him I understood. By now, Michael and the others were so far ahead I couldn't see them. 'Come on,' said Dad, 'I'll race you.' So we raced along the pavement, whooping and laughing like little kids. It was a cold night and our breath steamed in the air like dragons' smoke. I won, but only by nearly colliding into Michael's back like a six-foot cannonball.

I came back home full of noble intentions. I had rose-tinted plans for a Reconciliation Scene in which my mother and I would each beg the other's forgiveness and maybe shed tender tears in each other's arms. Unfortunately, when I arrived in the kitchen for breakfast, I found my mother preparing to go out to a 'baby shower' for the editor of *Venus* magazine. (Apparently this is when you give presents to someone who's pregnant, rather than waiting outside to see a light smattering of infants fall from the sky.) My mother was nursing a terrible suspicion that the presenter of *Rags To Riches* had bought the same gift as she had, a pure crystal baby-food jar with (personalized) porcelain lid. The strain of this suspicion cast a shadow on the morning, and when I reached for the waffles and maple syrup she gave me a lecture on the perils of comfort eating. It only leads to bigger trouser sizes and thus more misery: a 'vicious circle', she warned me darkly. Then she informed me that we were going for tea with Lord C-C that afternoon and that I'd better work on my maths assignment in the meantime. And get my hair cut.

By the time she left I was fuming again. Now that the unnaturally strained politeness between us appeared to be over it was as if my outburst had never been. Would it actually have killed her to just once ask me about Dad? Enquire how the evening had gone? Maybe even ask if Michael had enjoyed himself? She certainly hadn't given the impression of being 'ready to listen', whatever Dad might like to think . . . And so here we were with yet another hypocritical sucking-up session with Lord Snooty to look forward to. He was more of a health hazard than a couple of waffles in syrup. So what if I had shaggy hair and a bigger trouser size? Maybe I'd find a new boyfriend who'd love me for my inner beauty alone and we'd waddle off for long, romantic walks in matching tracksuit bottoms whilst feeding each other with yogurt-coated banana chips. That would show her.

In defiance of the 'vicious circle' warning I went out to get some chocolate supplies, although I resisted the temptation to look at newspaper reports on the Quicksilver Global Music Awards. When I got back I found a message on the answerphone from Dad. He said that he didn't know if I'd noticed, but the little art-house cinema in Brook Green was showing a themed series of films ('the garden in celluloid') and if I hadn't already made plans for the weekend I might like to take a look at the Hector Cleeve contribution. I went to look in the paper and there it was, Dad's debut feature, *The Keeper*, listed alongside some French and Japanese films I'd never heard of. I didn't know much about it, though I supposed that I must surely have seen it at some point since it was my mother's first screen appearance as well as my father's first film. I was probably too young for it to have made much of an impression on me, or perhaps my mother had censored it, considering this early per-formance to detract from her status as America's favourite English aristocrat. As it was showing on Sunday morning and was short – not quite an hour and a half – I decided I'd make the effort to go.

Lady Jane got back late from the baby shower, looking tired and out of sorts. I took it that the worst had happened and hers was not the only personalized crystal baby-food jar displayed on the expectant mother's gift stand. At least she didn't say anything about my untrimmed hair. Neither of us was in the best of moods as we set off for His Lordship's tea party and I expect that both of us uttered a silent prayer or two that today would be one of his better days.

It wasn't. Within the first two minutes I knew that this was going to be a special trial. All the surfaces in the drawing room were strewn with newspaper clippings and thick monogrammed paper covered in underscored paragraphs of brown ink – clearly those damned pinko liberals or the mafia-who-run-Europe had been up to something of which His Lordship disapproved and he was venting his fury in a series of poison pen letters. A favourite occupation of his and one that never failed to put a spring in his step, his cold black eyes snapping with malice.

Marie stalked in with a tray of cold, rubbery crumpets, each pasted with inch-thick butter, and a pot of weak tea for my grandfather and me. Five minutes later she came in with another cup for my mother, stewed nearly black because, as His Lordship remarked jovially, 'We know how you Northerners like your tea – dark as a coalmine, eh, Helen?' My mother didn't bother to respond, but sat very still and straight in the furthest corner from Lord C-C, tea untasted, a faraway look in her eyes. Perhaps she'd given up on her usual tactic of saintly compliance and was trying a different approach: strategic retreat. I wished I could do the same, but with my mother refusing to play the game, my grandfather turned his attention to me.

'Tell me, Octavia, have you seen anything further of the dashing young gentleman with whom you graced the pages of that society rag?'

I mumbled something about deciding that we weren't right for each other.

'Oh dear. *What* a pity. But I cannot help thinking that the romantic prospects of young ladies today have been materially damaged by certain deluded and unhappy women – they call themselves "feminists", you know – who still insist on peddling the most unsound ideas. The kind that only encourage dissatisfaction, recklessness and ingratitude. I do hope you have not fallen victim to this particular brand of *fussiness*?'

'Fussiness?' I asked weakly.

'Indeed. Now, I know nothing about the gentleman concerned, but I trust that you would not allow your social prospects to be damaged just because he fell short of some kind of sentimental or –' he shuddered '– *ideological* ideal. You are turning into a personable girl, but even so I do not think it is prudent to be unduly . . . shall we say *choosy* about such things.'

I sensed, rather than heard, my mother stir in her corner. I wished Viv was here to provide me with some snappy comeback line but kept quiet, despising myself for my cowardice.

'Octavia, my dear, perhaps I have been a little blunt. You must indulge a fond grandparent's concern. I am sure you might *eventually* find a young man to your liking.' He mused silently for a few moments. 'Although I suppose it could well be that you were wise not to pursue the connection with young Alexis further. As I recall, he had some association with the modern music business.' Pause. 'Which, like other artistic industries I could mention, has unhappily become the haunt of many foolish and immoral people.' His lip curled with distaste. 'Communists and homosexuals and the like.'

There was the sound of smashing china. My mother's teacup had fallen to the floor. She stood up, eyes glittering, and her voice was high and proud.

'That is enough. We will not listen to this any longer. You are a nasty, disgusting and absurd old man.'

My grandfather and I stared at her, transfixed. I think his mouth was actually hanging open with astonishment.

'You've been indulged and flattered and deferred to all your life by people who should know better, myself included. I don't know why anyone puts up with pathetic bullies like you. I don't know why I have, but it makes me ashamed.' She walked over from the couch with light, quick, determined steps and stood looking down at him. He shrank back into his chair in spite of himself. 'And do you know something, My Lord? You're a common little man. Common as muck, just like all those other people who haven't done anything with their lives except look down on everyone else. The only thing you have to command are your dirty little prejudices, and they'll always come cheap.' She swept to the door. 'Come along, Octavia.'

And she swept out of the house, slamming the front door behind us in Marie's scandalized face, and swept into the car and drove home at a highly illegal speed, all in a white-hot silence. When we got to our building she went up the stairs before me, still without speaking, went into her bedroom and shut the door and didn't come out all evening.

The next morning she must have left the house very early, for I woke at about half-past seven to an empty flat. Her note simply read 'back late'. She hadn't taken her phone with her and the car was still outside, left at the crooked angle she'd parked it last evening. I felt anxious and guilty and at a loss. There were so many things I wanted to say to her but last night, standing outside that closed, silent door, I hadn't known how to start. I just hovered for ages, waiting for the right words, the right gesture, to come, and when they didn't I was too ashamed to try. I thought of phoning Dad, but he never, ever mentions his estranged father and I'd always thought of it as a closed topic. Besides, I sensed that this was something my mother and I had to sort out by ourselves.

There was no point hanging around all day working myself into a state while I waited for my mother to come back, so I decided I might as well go and see Dad's film. I quite liked the idea of retreating to somewhere dark and warm and private where I could sit back and forget about things. The art-house cinema turned out to be a small, musty place with a broken Coke machine in the lobby, tattered salmon-coloured plush on the seats and only three other people in the auditorium, one of whom started snoring gently as soon as the lights went down.

From the opening credits, you could see that *The Keeper* was a shot-on-a-shoestring, fairly amateur effort.

Unsteady hand-held camera shots and scratchy sound recording gave it a home-made feel, while the cast, crew and locations had clearly been kept to the bare minimum. But you could also soon see why it got Dad noticed, kick-started his career, you might say. It's the story of a day in the life of a warden at a London park, who finds a young woman sleeping rough on a bench. Nothing much happens, exactly; it's more a character study than a narrative, as each person gets drawn further, reluctantly, into the other's world. The keeper is a middle-aged, humourless, lonely man (played by a now well-known character actor) who's come to despise the dreary uniformity of the park he tends. The young runaway is, of course, my eighteen-year-old mother.

I don't quite know what I expected. It wasn't a revelation in terms of her acting ability – the rawness and awkwardness of her delivery rang true not so much because it was a clever performance but because you didn't think of it as an 'act', even the fact that she was sometimes a little stilted, a little clumsy, was right for the part. No, what made my breath catch in my throat was how familiar and yet how strange this girl was to me, this Helen Slater with her Geordie accent soft and stumbling, her bitten fingernails and scraped-back hair, her thin, heart-shaped face bare of make-up, all fragile cheekbones and taut, pale skin. I imagined what my father must have felt as he coached her with her lines, coaxed her through her performance step by step, tried to make her relax, laugh maybe, all the while watching, *hoping*, as she brought to life this character he'd created and had such ambitions for. I imagined how he must have seemed to her, too: energetic and confident, fresh out of Oxford, with his public-school charm and clever, glamorous friends.

I sat alone in the cinema long after the end credits had rolled and the lights came back on. Eventually the woman at the ticket office came in to push an ancient vacuum cleaner around and I got chucked out. I felt light-headed and couldn't tell whether I was happy or sad; it was a bit like being drunk. When I got home I flicked through all the channels until I found an ancient *Lady Jane* repeat. I couldn't remember the last time I'd sat down and watched an episode right through, paying proper attention to it all, and I'd forgotten how entertaining it is. They've got loads of snappy, well-paid writers, of course, but it isn't just the script. My mother is *good*. Her comic timing, the way she twitches an eyebrow in a politely puzzled sort of way that's one of her trademarks, the sparkle in her eye like she's sharing the joke with the audience . . . the whole thing looks like fun. It was while I was laughing at the final punchline that my mother walked in the door.

We stood looking at one another. She must have gone for a walk in a park somewhere; it was a damp sort of day and there was mud and bits of leaf mould on her trousers. Her hair was straggling about her face, and although the exercise had put colour in her cheeks she looked red-eyed and wan. 'Octavia,' she said, 'I'm so sorry.'

I stared at her in bewilderment. '*You're* sorry? No, Mum, it's me. I'm the one who's—'

But she was already going on, in a strained, formal kind of voice. 'Lord Clairbrook-Cleeve is your only living relative apart from your father and me, so I have tried to honour the relationship between you. I know you find him difficult, God knows I do. Nonetheless, I wanted . . . I tried . . . to do the right thing by both of you. But yesterday—'

This time it was my turn to interrupt. 'Mum, stop. I love what you did yesterday. I want to *thank* you. I didn't know what to do and you were so . . . heroic. You rescued us.'

My mother flushed shyly. 'Really? Truly? You didn't mind?' I nodded vigorously, but she was looking troubled again, twisting her scarf in her hands. 'It's not just my outburst yesterday I have to apologize for. You see, the things I wanted so badly and found so difficult when I was your age – well, I wanted them to come effortlessly to you. I wanted you to be able to hold your own with people like your grandfather or India or Alexis or whoever you wished. I wanted you to have the means, to reach the position, of never feeling intimidated by anyone. And so whenever you seemed hesitant or . . . or *doubtful,* I thought all you were looking for was encouragement. Confidence. I was so determined not to let anything or anyone stand in your way I never took the trouble to find out which way you were actually going.'

'I understand. I do. I shouldn't ever have thrown a tantrum like I did last week, because I *am* grateful. I've enjoyed dressing up and going out to meet glamorous people and feeling attractive and confident . . . it's just that . . . well, sometimes being like that makes me feel worse about myself, not better.' I paused for a moment to find the right words. 'I don't think it's because of lack of practice. It's because I need something different, something . . . true to me, I suppose. That's why things could never work out with Alex, why Jess likes me and India despises me, why I love Michael, why I'm best friends with Viv, why I want to go to a normal school, have a normal career one day. All of those things.' I smiled at her. 'You once said that living an ordinary life isn't difficult. Well, I'm not so sure about that or even what an "ordinary life" means, if there is such a thing . . . I don't think I'll be taking the easy way out, you see, but I need to find out for myself. On my own terms.'

'Yes,' said my mother slowly. 'Yes. You're right. You tried to tell me last week . . . after Alex . . . and I thought I understood. I didn't know what to do, how to put things right, though. I still didn't see how I'd managed to get everything so wrong.' She took a deep breath. 'But then there was your grandfather yesterday, and as I was sitting there, listening to that absurd old man and his stupid, spiteful way of looking at the world, well, I was suddenly afraid you'd think I'm like that too. That I've been putting you under the same sort of pressures. That actually Lord Cleeve and I have come dangerously close to caring about the same things. And that makes me deeply ashamed and very, very sorry.'

I came up and put my arms around her. I felt her cheek against my neck and it was wet. 'Mum, don't, please don't. You and my grandfather are nothing alike, I know that, I really do. I've been a brat lately, not knowing what I wanted and then wriggling away from the responsibility by blaming you. I was so proud of you yesterday. Don't cry.'

It was a bit like the rose-tinted Reconciliation Scene

I'd planned on Saturday morning, except for the fact that I'd forgotten the amount of snotty tissues and hiccups generated by a good cry. But Saturday morning seemed like a different age and once we'd mopped up with tissues and suppressed the hiccups we sat down to finish up the waffles and maple syrup. Even after the inroads I'd made yesterday, there was a whole pack left.

And so we all lived happily ever after and Mum never made another remark about How To Make Friends And Influence People through the use of flawlessly applied nail polish and reduced-fat spread. Never again did I feel the urge to curl my lip or roll my eyes or slam my door in a self-righteous huff.

Well, not quite.

I'm afraid we still baffle and exasperate each other on a regular basis – it just doesn't seem all that important any more. Things between her and my father are a lot better too; she and Dad and Michael aren't about to have a group hug round the kitchen table, but at least Mum makes an effort to ask after them occasionally and even says hello to Michael when she comes to pick me up. She's on particularly good form at the moment, having just been contracted by Channel Five to present a lavish series on the history of the British aristocracy. Lord Clairbrook-Cleeve must be choking on his crumpets with rage. At least I hope so.

Dad's film has its American premiere next month and me, Jess and Viv are flying out to New York to attend it. They've decided to release the film there first, rather than in London, since America is currently in the grip of a fresh wave of Drake Montague mania after his first book of poetry was published to gushing acclaim. The dedication on the front page reads 'for Jezabel', but whether even the most well-balanced, down-to-earth man in the world could bask in Drake's current level of adulation and still keep his sanity remains to be seen. Jess just shrugs and smiles, a little wistfully.

I haven't seen Alex since our split, unless you count his regular appearances in society and gossip magazines. He is always pictured wearing a slightly glazed expression and with a glamorous girl hanging off his arm, though WeeWee has set her sights somewhat higher and is rumoured to be going out with Prince Richard.

India never came back to school after the Friday of Michael's birthday party, so I never found out what, if any, act of vengeance she was planning for me. According to Calypso, Cosmo, whose father produces the Vince Valiant films, pulled the necessary strings for India to land a part in the forthcoming blockbuster and her subsequent 'filming commitments' have sadly prevented her from finishing her education at Darlinham House (or from fulfilling her alleged contract with Cosmo, rumoured to involve an indecent act in the school toilets). Calypso is very bitter because *her* actress mother is something of a Vince Valiant institution, so she thinks the part should have gone to her. The film will not be released until next year, but I am quite looking forward to it. Apparently India spends most of her screen time either bound and gagged in a corner or running through sewers, screaming.

I'm leaving Darlinham House myself at the end of the year for Viv's comprehensive. Jess is leaving for a different school, but I definitely mean to keep in touch, especially now that Viv has a boyfriend who she is busy training to be an equal-opportunities activist. I try hard to be pleased for her, but sometimes I wish that once I'd done the right thing and rejected Mr Sexy-but-Shallow I could have fallen straight into the arms of my rightful reward, Mr Sexy-yet-Sincere, just like the loathsome Tammy did. But I don't regret either going out with Alex or breaking up with him, and when I remember the good moments – and there *were* a few – I suppose I'm . . . grateful.

So there we are. Soon I'll be in a new school among new people to whom any reference to D-list Dave or the Obelisk will be meaningless. They won't know my past incarnations as an amateur It-girl or dysfunctional Darling or A-list wannabe, or if I ever really fitted any of these labels and nicknames. I guess they're free to discover them for themselves or make up some new ones for me to disown or aspire to. Either way I'm not bothered, because Octavia Clairbrook-Cleeve can be all these things or none of them. It's up to me.